Second Chances and Then Some

A Novel

G.T. London

MAVITAE
Publishing

Dedicated to my husband, Jason—my partner-in-adventure, as well as my inspiration and my guide, without whom I would not dare to fly.

Contents

Prologue

Present day

I press my teeth hard into my lip, feeling a sharp pinch and tasting a metallic tang.

I bring the back of my hand to my mouth, smearing the blood.

Fear washes over me, and a bolt of pain shoots through my body.

I hurt people, and I may have killed people.

I did it again.

Chapter One

Seven months earlier

I sense his gaze, and as I turn my head, I notice that the man is looking at my phone screen over my shoulder with a smirk. I scowl at him.

"Pardon me," I say. My face flushes as the rest of the customers in line at the café look at me. The words came out louder than I'd intended.

I lower my voice. "People's phones are private and personal."

"Whoops, my bad." He takes a step back, raising his hand defensively. "I didn't mean to offend you."

Still scowling, I turn back to my phone, my hair whipping around me. Just then, a barista arrives at the counter to take my order. His eyes twinkle with his smile, and I'm grateful to see a friendly face.

"What can I get you?"

"A cortado with whole milk, please," I reply.

Pages and Beans is a small, gorgeous café in a historic

brick plaza. In the corner, there's a stack of books and a couple of upholstered armchairs below a vintage-looking PAGES sign. The delicious scent of coffee lingers in every nook. Finding the independent coffee shop close to my new job is an act of kindness to myself. I don't give myself many.

I feel sheepish about my outburst, but I know the feeling will fade once I sip the magical espresso with steamed milk. As I wait, out of the corner of my eye I see the man ordering a large latte with skimmed milk. Despite the café's thick aromas, I can still smell his strong cologne. He's tall and wears an expensive-looking winter coat. As he finishes ordering, I feel his gaze on me. Then he shoots a look at the barista before he leaves the café. What that look means I don't know, but I'm in too much of a hurry to worry about it.

This is my first day at my new position. I'm a temp and usually stay only a few weeks at each job.

"Here's your cortado—it's on the house." The barista beams, and before I can refuse, he leans forward and whispers, "This is a special cortado to make your day better. It's not on the usual menu. Hope you have a wonderful week."

"Thank you."

I'm still smiling minutes later as I stroll down the narrow street, heading toward my office building. It's remarkable how quickly one person can make you feel down and another can uplift you.

Suddenly worried that I'm going to be late, I accelerate

my pace. The street is longer than it looks. I hurry toward the massive office building that houses Thames City Healthcare Group headquarters. I'll be working for this prominent healthcare provider, whose outpatient clinics are spread throughout the country.

As soon as I enter the building, I'm in awe. It's an impressive triangle structure made entirely of glass. The abundance of natural light forces me to blink repeatedly. I rush into the full elevator and it begins moving before I can press the button for my desired floor. I search for the controls but find none.

"It's one of those elevators where you press the buttons before entering," says a woman. "So you'll have to go back to the lobby."

I force a smile. "Thank you."

Although the elevator stops at several floors, it unfortunately doesn't stop at mine. Only after everyone else has exited does it return to the lobby. All my attempts to make a good first impression with my clothes, hair, and makeup will be worthless if I don't get to the office by 8:30 a.m., and I'm cutting it close.

Once I'm on the way to the right floor, I notice my shoulders have stiffened like a board. I try to loosen them by moving them up and down. Finally, the elevator stops on the seventeenth floor, and I emerge into a modern reception area. The smooth white walls complement the sleek gray flooring and reflect the natural light pouring in through the expansive windows overlooking the city below.

I jerk to a stop when I see the tall guy from the café chatting with the receptionist. Hot coffee sloshes onto my hand.

Please go. Don't turn around—go.

My internal plea works, and he walks off without turning around. I exhale a long breath of relief.

Fixing a warm expression on my face, I walk toward the receptionist.

"Hello, I'm here to see Sarah, please."

She welcomes me, radiating professionalism.

My palm is sticky with the milky coffee. I dig around in my handbag for a tissue while the receptionist tells me Sarah will meet me soon. Just as I'm about to inquire where the ladies' room is, the receptionist gestures toward a woman walking down the corridor and says, "There she is."

I quickly wipe my hand with the electricity bill in my purse.

Sarah approaches with a gentle smile. "Ah, you must be Dasia. Welcome, my dear. I'm Sarah."

She holds out her hand. I hope she doesn't feel the stickiness on mine as we shake. She doesn't seem to notice.

"This way, Dasia," she says, beckoning.

We walk to her office, and as soon as we step inside I'm transfixed by the floor-to-ceiling windows, which showcase a sweeping view of the city. We're perched high above a bustling train station.

Sarah notices my admiration. "Quite a spectacular

view, right?" She indicates I should take a seat in a chair in front of her desk.

"It's like a natural extension of the urban landscape," I say.

"Have you had to travel far to get here?" She tucks her ash-gray hair behind her ear, and it's hard not to notice her effortless elegance.

"I live in North London."

"Ah, the leafy North London. I live in Hertfordshire."

"That's a long commute." I feel for Sarah. I live at the last station on my Tube line, and it's a long and challenging commute to the city center. Hertfordshire is even farther.

"I stay in London during the week."

"Ah, I see."

"I'm very happy to have you here, Dasia. Dasia—what a beautiful name, by the way. Let me give you some details about the job. I'm the newly appointed chief operations officer. You'll be supporting another executive leader and me. I'll introduce you to Charlene, the CEO's executive assistant. I'm sure she'll tell you everything you need to know about the building, the office, and the staff."

I've held over thirty jobs in the last two years, and Sarah is the warmest boss I've met. After she's walked me through my basic duties, she takes me to meet Charlene, who happens to sit just outside Sarah's office. There's a vacant desk adjacent to hers.

"Hi, I'm Charlene, Mr. Goodwin's EA," Charlene says in a cheerful tone, as she rises and extends her hand.

"I'm Dasia. Nice to meet you." I quickly shake her hand. I really need to refrain from shaking any more hands until I wash off the coffee residue.

With a gleam in her eye, Charlene gestures for me to sit at the desk beside hers. Both are in a small area in front of the executives' offices. She gives me an orientation and goes into more detail about my duties. Then I spend the morning poring over critical company policies and ticking off boxes on online checklists outlining health-and-safety protocols. Despite being someone who finds solace in lists, I find these ones dull and repetitive, so I take periodic breaks to admire the bird's-eye view of the city.

Around midday, I make my way to the office kitchen. I catch the sound of footsteps and quickly turn around to see who's behind me. Once again, it's the man from the café. He brushes past me and pours himself a glass of water then turns around and studies me for a second. I'm stunned when, without a word, he steps toward me and leans in, fixing his gaze on the right side of my face. I flinch.

"You have something brown on your jaw," he says, and strolls out of the kitchen.

I rush to the ladies' room. The lighting isn't the friendliest, but I can see that I missed a small spot of the beautifying mask I used the night before. My eyes burn, and tears gather on my eyelashes. I'm furious with myself.

Shaking my head, I blink hard. Then I straighten my posture, position my legs shoulder-width apart, and place my hands on my waist. I'm going for the Wonder Woman stance. I take deep breaths, in and out.

Let's start again, Dasia.

"Give today another chance," I say out loud. I already feel better.

Looking at myself in the mirror, I smooth my dark-brown hair. It's silky and shiny and falls just below my shoulders. I take one more deep breath and then step out of the bathroom, determined to forget about the tall man's rude behavior.

The afternoon passes uneventfully, although I get lost several times in the mazelike corridors. Charlene buzzes about, scheduling meetings, coordinating travel plans, and efficiently handling other administrative tasks.

Finally, I leave the office building and welcome the late-afternoon breeze that touches my face. Although it's not terribly cold, I can't help but feel a chill run through me. Something about this first day has felt strange—and I'm not quite sure why.

Chapter Two

When I get home almost an hour later, my gaze darts around my space. My bedroom, living room, and dining room are all the same room. I sigh and look at the pile of clothes on my bed —skirts, trousers, blouses, and dresses. I'm twenty-nine years old and live in a small apartment that I share with two strangers. My bedroom is the center of my world in this life I've set out to live. A life of solitude. This way, I can't inflict further pain on anyone else.

My dress feels tight around my chest. It's a black midi dress with a metal-work-belted waist, a V-neck, and three-quarter sleeves. It usually makes me feel confident. But it didn't do the trick today. I feel unsettled after my encounters with the tall man.

I light a jasmine candle, but the calming scent wafting through the air doesn't soothe me. I decide to start a checklist. Checklists always comfort me—no matter how long or short they are. I love the act of jotting down a task and the joy I feel when I cross it off the list. Today, I have just one action item.

- Erase the memory of the tall man with the distractingly handsome face and his discourteous behavior at the café and in the office kitchen.

Satisfied, I grin as I check off the item.

I then search my purse for the electricity bill. I was appalled when I looked at it this morning on my way to work. I can't fathom why the bill has nearly doubled over the past month. I'm always surprised that utilities cost so much. It's shocking, really.

I need to discuss the cost-sharing arrangement with my roommates. They work from home and use far more electricity. I jolt at the shrill wail of a siren. An emergency vehicle speeds down the busy road my bedroom looks out on. I wonder who might be hurt. I try not to think about those I've hurt.

The next morning, as I emerge from the Underground station, I inhale cold air into my lungs and adjust my scarf so that it's appropriately draped across my shoulders. I need to buy some gloves—the cold is already taking its toll on my hands, and I can't put them in my pockets right now because I'm carrying my coffee maker. I plan to claim a small corner of the office kitchen and create a coffee station.

At the office, I immediately head to the kitchen to set up the machine and place a package of ground coffee in the cabinet. Then I walk to my desk and settle into my chair to watch the busy Londoners below, rushing to work. I love the view, but I know better than to get too comfortable here. I take only entry-level temp jobs and stay for a few weeks. In the last two years, I've worked at a publishing company, a GP's office, an insurance brokerage, a translating service, a cleaning operation, and a web-based retail company. There seems to be a constant need for temporary office assistants.

This contract is for four weeks; I'll finish up just before Christmas, which isn't exactly an ideal time to look for another temporary position. But I'll cross that bridge when I get to it.

Yesterday, Charlene asked me several questions, but I've learned how to tactfully deflect inquiries without seeming impolite. I kept my responses brief and concise while avoiding eye contact.

"How long are you here for?"

"Four weeks."

"Ah, that's too short. We'll miss you when you go."

No, you won't miss me, Miss Chatterbox!

Charlene looked at me curiously when I didn't

respond. Then she turned her bright eyes back to her screen and continued typing away.

I'm not on social media, so I'll cease to exist in Charlene's world when I complete my contract. The people at this office will never know the real me. They'll never know my secret, which haunts me every day and keeps me imprisoned in my solitary life.

As I'm taking off my walking shoes and putting on my office heels, Sarah appears in the corridor. "Good morning, Dasia," she says, standing by her office door. "Once you settle into the day, let's do some introductions."

"Sure, that'll be great."

Ten minutes later, Sarah and I walk into a large open space filled with desks. She leads me to one of them.

"Emilia, meet Dasia. Emilia is our HR manager."

Emilia looks up and extends her hand without getting out of her chair. "Hi, I'm Emilia," she says briskly. Her tone isn't friendly.

I take her hand. "I'm Dasia."

"Sarah, I meant to ask you, can we talk about the critical issue I emailed you about yesterday?" She fixes her gaze on my boss. Emilia's fair skin is a stark contrast to her dark hair cascading down in waves. She's beautiful and clearly a pro at applying makeup, but I can't help but notice one eyelash missing from her extensions.

"Yes, I'll get back to you on that once I introduce Dasia to the rest of the team."

Sarah and I continue our walk and stop by a small office. My chest tightens.

Uh-oh, here he is again.

The tall man from yesterday.

"Luke, let me introduce you to Dasia," says Sarah.

As he rises from his chair, I detect a subtle upturn of his lips at the corners, a tiny mischievous grin.

"Hello, Dasia." His unwavering stare makes me uneasy, and his grip feels strong when I shake his hand.

"Nice meeting you," I mumble. My gaze settles on the floor. I can't look into people's eyes when I lie.

"Nice meeting you, too," he says, with a hint of playfulness. Once again I have that unsettling feeling.

"You'll be supporting Luke and me," Sarah says.

Oh no. So this is the other executive leader—and we've gotten off to a terrible start. I give him a tight smile. When we leave his office, I resist the urge to break into a sprint. I'm relieved when I'm back at my desk and alone once again.

"Did you meet everyone?" Charlene asks, when she returns after her morning meetings.

"Yes, I did."

"How about Luke? What did you think of him?"

"Yeah, I met him." Unfortunately, it seems that maintaining a distance from Charlene will prove to be a difficult task. "He seems okay."

"Come on." Her *n* is long and drawn out, as if it's dripping thick molasses. Charlene leans closer and continues. "Let me tell you a secret. He's single, but rumor has it he's unavailable. Maybe he's in a secret relationship, or he doesn't do serious relationships. I'm inclined to believe the former."

A chatterbox colleague is my worst nightmare. Chatterbox Charlene has an angular face, moves quickly, and talks animatedly, as if she always has a secret to tell. Her eyes constantly roam the office, and her full rimmed glasses with a touch of blue add a distinct air of superiority that instantly lets people know she is not one to mess with.

"I need to set up a meeting for Mr. Goodwin," she says. "He has a reputation for his short temper. See you later." She grabs her notepad and disappears into the corridor. I take a deep breath, but before I can even exhale, I see Luke walking toward my desk with his effortless gait.

He locks his gaze on the corner of my desk, and I realize he's looking at my phone. "That's a movie-theater-sized phone."

I scowl at him. Again. Third time in less than forty-eight hours.

He winks. "Your secret is safe with me." He walks off.

My body feels as if it's made of ice, ready to shatter at any moment. How could he possibly know my secret?

I don't know how long I sit still as I try to grasp the gravity of the situation. I replay the moment over and over. So, he winked. Maybe that was actually an eye twitch? But a corner of his lip moved upward, forming an unmistakable smirk. *Oh my. He knows. How?*

This is only my second day, and I'm already made. I sit and stare at my screen as the clock ticks away.

"Here's a confession I haven't shared with anyone

else." His mocking voice startles me as he appears next to my desk—again. He's standing far too close for my liking.

I stare at him, narrowing my eyes, unyielding. He shifts uncomfortably.

"Listen, I loved watching those too and haven't seen one for years. I was just curious."

My eyebrows shoot up in surprise and confusion. "Huh?"

"*The Love Boat!*"

As all the tension drains out of me, I can't help but close my eyes briefly in relief. He doesn't know my secret —that's what matters. He's referring to what he saw on my phone screen at the café yesterday: a classic episode of *The Love Boat*, from the 1980s.

"I was only trying to see which episode you were watching," he says, his expression apologetic. "I wasn't trying to invade your personal space."

As he vanishes into the corridor, another wave of relief washes over me. I realize how foolish I'd been to misinterpret his words.

"Just relax!" I whisper to myself, fully aware of the absurdity of the notion, considering my perpetual state of unease.

Chapter Three

I'm happy it's finally Friday. Following the unsettling excitement of my first couple of days, the remainder of my week has passed like any other typical workweek.

My tasks are monotonous. I support Sarah in her administrative activities, and I also helped her with a few tech issues this week. One of my primary responsibilities is to support the meetings. Today is my first meeting in this role, and the meeting chair is Luke.

I always book fifteen minutes of preparation time before a meeting so I can access the room and check that everything is in place and ready to go. I love planning and preparing—knowing what's ahead of me. Initially, this made working for a temping agency a nerve-racking experience, but I adapted and eventually settled into a rhythm. Now, each of my short contracts feels like an adventure, and I take pride in my ability to be spontaneous.

Perhaps I should create a checklist for how to be spontaneous. How silly that would be.

After I've projected the agenda onto the screen and checked all the technology, ensuring everything works, I take a seat facing the city and once again admire the view.

A few minutes before the meeting, attendees start pouring in, talking among themselves. Emilia's laughter fills the air.

So, she is friendly and joyful—around certain people.

There are twelve attendees. Four join the meeting virtually and eight in person, including Luke. Luke arrives last, and as he enters, the energy in the room changes. I see respect in the attendees' expressions. He takes the empty chair next to Emilia, and they eye each other for a beat.

Luke wears a crisp white neatly pressed shirt. It had to have been dry-cleaned. I can't imagine him turning a slightly damp shirt inside out and holding a steam iron to it, starting with the back of the collar, humming a bright song. Although it's something I'd love to see.

Luke starts the meeting with a message from Mr. Arthur Goodwin. I haven't met the company's new CEO, but I've heard his nickname: the Iron Fist. As the meeting progresses, Luke challenges the team. "We can do this. There are many cost-saving measures we can take."

"You mean like layoffs," someone says.

"Yes, like layoffs, too. But there're ways to avoid job losses." His gaze sweeps around the table, and then he looks at the screen.

Almost everyone nods.

Then Luke startles me by leaning over my arm and grabbing the remote control. He looks at me for only a split second, but I catch his eyes widening slightly. It's an intense look that suggests he wants to know more, to explore the unknown. Raising my chin, I attempt to conceal the faint shiver moving through my body.

As Luke continues his presentation, sharing more graphs and numbers, I notice people continue nodding. I find myself slipping into memories of family dinners at the table when I was a child. My brother always nodded enthusiastically when my mother talked. I didn't say much when she spoke, but I don't know if she ever noticed my silence.

I shift my attention to the people who have been silent since the start of the meeting, pondering their backgrounds and stories. I can't help but wonder how they came to be at this table, where their voices remain unheard. What are their lives like beyond this meeting room? Do families wait for them at the end of their workdays? How do they interact around their dinner tables?

As the meeting comes to a close, I prepare to leave the office and then head home to the dinner table in my bedroom. It has only one chair. My rented room is in a first-floor apartment, within a charming three-story Victorian terraced house, which shares its walls with its neighbors'. On the opposite side of my paper-thin wall, there may be a family sitting down to supper right now.

Mostly, I hear only creaks and cracks coming from within the walls. The constant sounds lull me to sleep.

Hey brother,

Do you remember when we did that homemade-volcano experiment using baking soda, vinegar, and red food coloring to create a realistic eruption? And how we stupidly got caught by our parents? Every time I think about it, I can't help but laugh.

As we sat around the dinner table that night, we tried to act natural and innocent, tried not to giggle and nod at everything Mom and Dad said. I remember feeling a mix of excitement and nerves, nodding away, pretending that nothing was going on.

But then came the loud POP from your bedroom, and we all rushed in to find a massive cloud of baking soda, vinegar, and red food coloring spewed everywhere.

Remember how livid Mom was? But we thought we were actually two successful child scientists. Dad always encouraged us to explore and satisfy our curiosity but to do so together. I remember him winking at us, trying to calm Mom. But we both got grounded.

This morning, the muffled voices of my neighbors permeated the thin walls, hinting at something unusual unfolding on the other side; not sure what, though. Their mayhem reminded me of our own, brightening my morning with our memories.

Oh, how I miss you, Eli!

Sending you all my love.

Dasia

I press send and close the laptop, which sits on my small table. I write to my brother often and share whatever is on my mind. We're only eleven months apart, and growing up, we loved to show everyone that we were siblings. At school, he'd call out "Hey, sis!" and I'd beam, so proud that everyone knew that he was my brother. Only a few of us call him Eli, our beloved Elias.

After Dad passed away, my brother took over the family business—manufacturing toothpaste. He's focused on using natural ingredients and working with dentists and scientists to continually refine the product. He's a great leader and a fantastic businessman despite being only twenty-seven.

My brother was disappointed when I refused to join the family business after college. But I had my own dreams. I wanted to create software tools with assistive technologies to help people, and to develop autonomous systems that improved people's daily lives.

My mother's family has been in the toothpaste business for three generations, and they take great pride in this. My father had no interest in joining the business—he loved his hands-on job as an engineer. In the end, though, he had to join.

I held my ground, despite my brother's attempts to persuade me.

"Sis, just imagine how awesome it would be if we worked together! With your inventions and our determination, we could take the family business to the next level. And hey, you can pick any color for your hard hat!"

"Is that all you have to offer? You don't even wear those at work!"

My brother is always joking around. And he's always been the golden child in our family. "See how your brother impressed his teachers? Learn from him," my mother would say. Her voice continues to resonate within me while my frustration etches two deep wrinkles between my eyebrows. I refer to these lines as my "mother-Botox collection."

When parents play favorites, what happens to the other kid?

As children, my brother and I did everything together. We loved playing puzzle games, but my mother always insisted I let him win. "He's younger than you," she'd whisper in my ear. "Stop trying to outshine him."

I loved the puzzle games, but I loved my brother more, so I let him win every time. Now, after everything that happened, my brother is the only person who truly cares about me.

It's strange how memories can come flooding back so vividly in the present moment. I look around my bedroom. The contrast between my current living space and my cherished childhood home could not be starker.

It's been two years since I stumbled on this room. While I do share the bathroom and kitchen with my two roommates, my life remains a separate entity.

When I moved to London, I dreamed of attending musicals, enjoying ballet at the Royal Opera House, and splurging on scrumptious dinners created by award-winning chefs. Fast-forward two years, and I've managed to attend only a single musical with a last-minute, restricted-view ticket. I couldn't even see certain areas of the stage. Nevertheless, I found the experience magical.

But then, there is so much to do in this city, like visiting bookstores where I easily lose track of time. Just like stepping into the book market under Waterloo Bridge feels like discovering a hidden sanctuary where literary treasures await, and the best part is, there's no cost to enter —only endless value.

Earlier this morning I decided to make myself pancakes, a Saturday treat—my urge to write to my brother delayed my breakfast. The pancakes are perched on a plate beside me, their soft, fluffy texture and tantalizing aroma beckoning me closer. I eat all my meals at this small table.

"Yummy," I say out loud. A feeling of pure delight engulfs me when I bite into the buttery goodness. Another memory arrives.

"Dad, what if we make the pancake in the shape of New Jersey?"

Dad was used to my wild ideas, but my brother chuckled.

"That's silly, Dasia. We can't do that." Still, I attempted to cut my pancake into the shape of the state.

My brother laughed loudly. "Looks more like a mutant New Jersey."

My father had been a mechanical engineer, and he loved his job. "See those wind turbines, kids? Your old man makes the best-quality bolting application for those."

But everything changed the day he was laid off and forced to join the family business. Although he had a senior-leadership role in the business, he never showed much excitement for the work. And our wonderful pancake mornings became a distant memory when he started working long hours, pouring himself into his new role.

I remember being sad. I missed our breakfasts, and I missed spending time with him. I didn't understand the pressure he was under.

Chapter Four

Two weeks at my new job fly by. By Monday of week three, I've adjusted to my role and am maintaining a cordial, professional distance from others.

Just as I'm about to prepare for a 4:00 p.m. meeting, I notice Luke exiting his office and walking toward my desk, his hands deep in his pockets.

"Dasia," he says, as he gets closer.

"Luke," I respond, my eyes meeting his. It's a little game we've started playing, saying each other's names. No one seems to notice, yet the exchanges always feel weighty.

"Mr. Goodwin might join the meeting. Could you record it?"

"Say please," I whisper, unable to resist taking the jab. Isn't it a universal truth that Brits are famous for their love of *please* and *thank you*? Apparently, he didn't get that memo.

"Did you say something?" he asks.

"No, Luke," I say, standing. "I didn't say a thing. I'll record the meeting."

A tense silence settles between us.

"I'll get on it," I say, stepping away from his presence. I can feel his eyes on me. I don't look back, but I can't stop the surge of nervous energy coursing through me.

I practically sprint to the meeting room.

As I'm setting up, people start gathering around the oval-shaped meeting table. Emilia and Luke walk in together, followed by Sarah. I'm surprised to see her, as this meeting wasn't on her calendar, and Luke and Sarah don't usually attend these meetings together. She takes a chair across the table from Luke.

The afternoon sun is pouring in, so I lower the window shades.

Emilia blinks. It's hard not to notice how long her eyelashes are. "Don't block the sunshine, Dasia," she demands.

"We won't see the screen with the glare," I respond, trying to hide my irritation.

Luke gets up, walks toward the shades, and raises them —not entirely, but enough to impress Emilia. The chemistry between them is palpable. Their energy could heat the entire office building.

As Luke resumes his seat at the head of the table, I can't help but be struck by his commanding presence. He sits tall, and his expensive-looking blue suit molds to his body. He takes off his jacket. His broad shoulders fill out his crisp white shirt. His cuffs are round and have glossy cuff links. It's clear that he takes pride in his appearance.

He begins to speak. When deep in thought, he runs a hand through his well-groomed beard, which sports a few gray strands. His hair is a rich brown. Every aspect of his appearance adds to his confident presence.

I note that Sarah doesn't contribute but listens to Luke intently.

All heads simultaneously swivel toward the entrance when Mr. Goodwin walks in. He's wearing a dark suit. He probably thinks he looks sophisticated, but really, he appears a bit awkward as only one button of his jacket is properly fastened, and it sits right in the middle, stretching the jacket around his belly. He's also wearing his usual expression, the one that seems to say "You're fired."

He sits next to Luke. "Can we see the presentation on the screen?" He drums his thick fingers impatiently on the table. "I don't have all day." His small head bobs up and down slightly as he speaks.

I leap up and grab the remote control. "Here it is." I press the button, only to be met with a blank screen. With mounting apprehension, I press the button repeatedly, but the screen doesn't come to life.

"This is strange," I say nervously. "I checked it before the meeting. It was working."

"Obviously it hasn't been checked properly," Mr. Goodwin barks.

His dismissive comment makes my blood boil.

As Luke stands and walks toward the screen, I can feel that my cheeks are flushed and that people's gazes are dancing around me. Luke bends and picks up a cord to show that it's not plugged in. That's all. He plugs it in, and the presentation appears on the screen. I'm absolutely sure I plugged that cord into the socket fifteen minutes ago.

While he strides over to the presentation screen, he looks at me for a beat. His dark-brown dress shoes stand out against his blue suit. *This man's a walking contrast*, I think. *In both his inner and outer worlds.*

Luke restarts his presentation.

Afterward, Mr. Goodwin asks questions; no one else dares to talk. He then states, "The board is not happy." He draws out each word as excruciatingly slowly as a snail making its way across a hot, rough surface.

"The condition of our South London Outpatient Hospital is unfavorable. Budgetwise, it's been falling behind for the past two years, and the high turnover of staff is leading to critical situations. Additionally, the cost of agency staff is significantly exceeding the allocated budget." Mr. Goodwin pauses, looking around the room with a cold, calculating gaze.

"And don't even get me started on the inefficiencies. The operational processes within the hospital are riddled with them, resulting in delays and bottlenecks in patient care."

His voice gets even colder. The room feels chillier.

"Let me make myself perfectly clear: I demand nothing

short of unwavering dedication from each and every one of you to rectify this dire situation. There will be severe consequences if you don't rise to the occasion and do whatever it takes to reverse our current predicament. The choice is yours."

With that, he stands and leaves. And then chaos erupts. People start talking, interrupting one another, and the room fills with a jumbled mess of voices. I catch Luke and Sarah looking at each other with concern.

"Everyone, stop!" Luke booms in a deep voice.

There's a moment of stunned silence. Everyone stares at Luke. I can't help but be impressed.

"We're in this together," Sarah says. "Let's not panic." All eyes turn toward her as she rises. "We've got the skills and drive to devise a good plan," she says confidently. "We must keep working together and take it one step at a time."

Luke picks up where Sarah left off. Their display of unity is extraordinary. "Trust me, we can do this."

A fire burns in his eyes, a fierce determination that tells me he won't give up without a fight. But, as I watch him, I can tell he's worried. Despite his best efforts to hide his uneasiness, I can see right through him.

Chapter Five

A few days later, I push open the bathroom door and immediately hear someone sobbing. I suspect it might be Sarah, as I saw her enter the bathroom earlier. I hesitate, not sure if I should say something. The sobbing stops. Whoever is in the stall must be aware of my presence, but no one exits.

I return to my desk but keep glancing at the bathroom door. In the last few days, I've seen Sarah and Luke have several conversations and meetings. Sarah was in a good mood earlier. Did something just happen?

Sure enough, ten minutes later Sarah emerges from the bathroom with a fresh layer of powder on her face. She walks past my desk and steps into her office without a word.

Life happens. Coffee helps.

I head for the office kitchen. I need a treat not just for the taste buds but also for the mind and soul. I brought a bag of Hawaiian Kona coffee to the office this week. It's light and sweet and reminds me of the barista at Pages and Beans Café—both have the power to make my heart beat a little faster. In the past three weeks I've developed a bit of a crush on the barista. He's always so kind to me and has a charming twinkle in his eye.

Waving the barista from my thoughts, I turn my attention to the task at hand: making the perfect cup of coffee to lift Sarah's spirits. I prepare the brew carefully and then watch as each drop falls into the pot. The aroma fills my senses, and I can't help but hope it brings Sarah some comfort.

After pouring two cups, I take a sip and grin with pleasure, savoring the complex flavors—smokiness, fruitiness, earthiness, spiciness, and nuttiness—while the steam invades my nostrils.

Mugs in hands, I head to her office. "Sarah," I say, from her door, "I was making myself a coffee and made you one too."

"How lovely, Dasia. Come on in." She turns away from her computer screen.

I set the mug on a coaster on her desk. "Freshly ground coffee from Hawaiian coffee beans."

Sarah studies me for a moment. "Is it really from Hawaii?"

"Yes, from the Kona region on the Big Island," I say proudly.

Her face softens with a smile. "My husband and I spent

ten glorious days in Hawaii on our honeymoon, thirty-eight years ago."

She takes a sip, and the coffee seems to whisk her away to a happier place. She looks as if she can feel fine, warm sand slipping through her toes. "This is wonderful!"

"The coffee trees grow on volcanic and rocky soil," I say. I've always been impressed by the resilience and adaptability of the trees in the face of challenges.

"How do you know this?" asks Sarah.

"One summer, I worked as a barista for a local coffee shop. They were desperate for help. That's how my love affair started with the coffee beans. I researched and read so many books about them."

Something dings on Sarah's computer, and she glances at the screen. She clicks on a message and frowns. Standing next to her, I unintentionally see her screen:

```
All,
Urgent meeting in 15 minutes, in my
office.
A
```

"I've got a few things to do," I say, thinking I should give her space. "I'll get back to my desk."

"Please stay for a few minutes, Dasia. Have your coffee."

I sit, and we both sip our coffees. Her eyes brighten, and a calmer expression spreads on her face.

"Exactly what I needed." She smiles. She radiates a loving maternal energy even when she's upset. She stares at her coffee but continues to talk. "I've worked for this company longer than I've been married to my husband. I'm proud of my achievements and my new executive role."

She pauses then glances at me. "Did you know that I'm the only female executive-team member?" A glint of pride shines in her eyes.

"Really?" I say, impressed. "I had no idea."

Sarah looks out her window for a few seconds. "I've climbed quite a ladder," she says, then adds, "Did you know that I'm also the oldest executive-team member?"

"You mean the most experienced?" I ask, wondering where this conversation is heading.

Sarah takes another sip of coffee, and her eyelids close for a few seconds.

"I mean older. There's no point beating around the bush, Dasia. Older means older, and many other wonderful things." She smiles and continues. "The people who work here aren't just employees or staff members—they're an extension of my family. So the thought that they might lose their jobs and face an uncertain future is daunting. And at times," she says, her voice trembling slightly, "it gets to me."

I can't help but wonder why she's confiding in me. Maybe she's embarrassed that I heard her crying earlier.

She turns to look at a photo on her desk.

"They've got your smile," I say.

"They do. The twins, my grandchildren, they're my

42

world." Her smile reveals her love. "They're twelve, and I'm a proud g'ma."

"G'ma?"

"Yes, I'm their g'ma—their fun and young g'ma." Her kind blue eyes stare at the photo for another moment, and then she looks at me. "Thanks again for the coffee, Dasia. I'll take it with me to my next meeting and it'll help me get through it." Her warm smile crinkles the corners of her eyes.

I go back to my desk and watch her leave for the meeting, hoping that the coffee really does help her get through whatever it is the meeting holds.

Chapter Six

The meetings pile up as the week winds down. The team's mission is to figure out how to make the South London Outpatient Hospital more efficient. They're considering all the operational processes and procedures and how to make them better and faster.

I've just come out of a late-afternoon meeting, another urgent one, and my brain has been reduced to the size of a pea, so I start preparing for my commute home, thanking the universe that Friday is just around the corner.

"Shoot!" I mutter under my breath, remembering that I left the recording equipment in the meeting room—still running. I rush back but pause when I see Mr. Goodwin and Luke having a private conversation in the room. I walk back to my desk to wait. Luke won't be happy that I left the equipment in the room, but he doesn't have to know that it's recording their conversation.

Later, I'll delete their conversation without listening, I tell myself.

I hang around and steal glances at the glass-walled meeting room. I can see Mr. Goodwin pacing back and forth, his eyes darkening with anger, his posture hostile.

A few minutes later, they enter the corridor. I wait until they've disappeared down the hall before rising slowly from my chair. I glance around to ensure no one is watching. With steady movements, I balance an imaginary stack of books on my head and walk purposefully into the meeting room. Then, continuing to move slowly and appear composed, I deftly reach for the recording device on the shelf beneath the screen.

My grip is tight, my curiosity high as I walk back to my desk and sink into my chair. I look at the recording device. My mind is in turmoil. *Please don't do it. Don't listen to it, Dasia.*

I can't stop myself, though. I sit, put the earphones firmly in my ears, and transfer the recording to my computer. I should head home, but something's keeping me at the office. Something's compelling me to listen to the recording.

I press play and hear the opening conversation of our earlier meeting. I nearly jump out of my seat when Charlene returns and starts chirping at me, even though I have the earphones on.

"Any plan for the weekend, Dasia?"

"Nothing specific," I reply.

"Have a look at this. We're going here this weekend."

She motions to her computer screen. I gesture to my ears, indicating that I'm occupied. But she insists. As I go over to her desk, still listening to the meeting recording, I press fast-forward. Then I hear Mr. Goodwin's bitter voice.

"Son, you've nothing to be worried about. Work with me here."

My chest throbbing, I can't concentrate on what Charlene is showing me on her screen. I point at my ears again. "Sorry," I whisper.

My ears soak up every word, and I cross my arms tightly.

Mr. Goodwin goes on.

"We'll be firing 50 percent of its administrative workforce unless there's some sort of miracle." His tone lacks compassion. "I don't believe in miracles, Luke."

"Surely there are things we can do." Luke's deep voice carries a hint of unease.

"We'll see. But mark my words, this is only the beginning, and I don't think the hospital will be able to recover from this."

A tense silence descends. Then I hear Mr. Goodwin again.

"Here's a confidential report. It addresses the automation project you proposed to improve efficiencies. But, son, you've got to let another executive lead this."

I'm perplexed as to why Mr. Goodwin calls Luke son. And why would he insist on another leader for the project? There's silence. Luke must be peeking at the report.

"I believe I'm a better fit to lead it," Luke says,

sounding troubled. I wonder why. Perhaps he doesn't want anyone else to shine.

"Executive layoffs are inevitable, and it's almost certain that the executive who leads this project will lose their job. Do you get me? They'll be fired." Mr. Goodwin's voice is cold, and there's another heavy silence before he continues. "Hear me out. I'll suggest to the board that Sarah leads the project since she's the newest executive member—let's see if she's as good as everyone says. I think she's a long shot." More silence. I rush back to my desk.

"Look," Mr. Goodwin continues, in a caring tone that sounds forced, "I can see you're concerned about Sarah. But she's been working here for a long time. She'll have enough savings should she lose her job, right?"

Blood rushes to my head. *You can't do this!*

"Why are you shaking your head?" Charlene asks.

"Oh! Nothing."

I take a deep breath and continue listening to the recording.

"I work very closely with Sarah."

"Even better, son. Keep an eye on her. This particular hospital is a pain in every sense. The oldest in the company. Too rigid, too old to improve. I know some board members agree it's not even worth the trouble."

I widen my eyes so much it hurts.

"You're a leader with potential, Luke, and you're young. You'll learn. We'll achieve great things together."

48

I listen intently, hoping Luke will respond as a compassionate leader and a caring colleague, someone committed to looking out for a peer. I've been admiring how well he and Sarah work together.

But instead of saying something along the lines of "We'll improve the numbers and turn things around, Sarah is a fantastic leader, and the hospital will thrive again," Luke, the executive director of strategy and improvement, says nothing. A big fat nothing.

His silence saddens me deeply, and I feel weighed down. It's as if there's a delete button with Sarah's name on it and they're about to push it. The unfairness and injustice of it all is like a bucket of ice-cold water to the face.

Is Luke nodding along to all of this? Mr. Goodwin clearly favors him and doesn't like Sarah, and I can't believe that Luke would stoop so low to get ahead. The disappointment in my heart transforms into overwhelming anger.

Mr. Goodwin's final words send a shiver down my spine. "Let's keep this conversation between us, son."

With intense emotions surging through my veins, I remind myself that I'm finishing my contract in a week and should mind my own business. My hand hovers over the delete button and my lips tremble as a single tear drips onto my hand.

I can't do it. I can't press the button. Instead, I save the recording and turn off my screen.

Minutes later, as I join the throngs of people on the streets of London, questions run through my mind.

What if I can leverage the skills from my previous career to help Sarah with the automation project?

How much risk can I take?

How much risk is too much?

Chapter Seven

I'm not who I appear to be at work. My current CV reads:

Name: Dasia A. Harris
Computer skills: Beginner/ intermediate
Education: High school

In reality, I'm a computer science engineer who graduated with honors from my elite college, Massachusetts Institute of Technology, before I moved to the UK.

Immediately after graduation, I started working for a self-driving car manufacturer in their development and testing department. I was over the moon—building the technology for and helping to design a self-driving car was my dream job. I moved from assistant to lead computer-science engineer in a few years. I was developing cutting-edge algorithms that enabled cars to navigate safely and efficiently in complex environments. Specifically, I led the development of sensors and systems that could detect and respond to various obstacles and conditions on the road. I dreamed of being featured in international business and science magazines as the youngest computer-science engineer to design driverless cars. I imagined my mother finally being proud of me.

It all came crashing down when I received that fateful phone call. The shrill ring signaled the beginning of an avalanche of tragedies that would reduce my life to ruins.

I was at the office with my teammates when the call came.

"There's been a crash," said the operator of the self-driving car.

I whirled around, my eyes wide with shock. "There's been a crash," I repeated to my team members, my voice quivering with terror.

Everyone stopped what they were doing, fear etched into their faces. I felt as if my heart were trying to force its way out of my rib cage. For a few agonizing moments, no one spoke. We just stared at each other.

Finally, my assistant software engineer broke the eerie stillness. "I hope no one was hurt, Dasia."

I'd spoken to the operator before the test. "The car has state-of-the-art systems and sensors," I'd said, smiling proudly. "Just enjoy the ride. This is a tick-box exercise."

Yes, it was a tick-box exercise, but it was still a crucial test drive to ensure safety. I'd still been beaming with pride as I sent the operator off. I must have muddled his judgment. I'd led him to put too much trust in the technology. I should have known better.

The operator explained that the car had been driving in a construction zone and a pedestrian pushing a bicycle had appeared on the poorly lit, multilane road. Large bags hung from the bike's handlebars.

The self-driving car didn't recognize the pedestrian. Instead, the software registered the cyclist as a small vehicle and didn't alert the operator because it was programmed to let the driver take control under these circumstances. But in this case, the operator wasn't paying attention. He wasn't looking at the road. The car alerted him only two seconds before impact.

The operator hit the brake. But it was too late.

The vehicle hit the pedestrian pushing the bicycle, a bus crashed into the vehicle, and three other cars piled up behind the bus.

As I listened, I felt as if my throat were closing up, squeezing the air out of me. Every breath was a struggle.

I collapsed into my chair. "Oh, no," I murmured. "No." *I might have killed people.*

The events of that day have haunted my memory ever since. My pride and my soul were both mercilessly crushed in the wake of the disaster.

After being in a coma for three months and three days, the cyclist pulled through. But I knew her life would never be the same. Two other people were hospitalized with non-life-threatening injuries.

The driver was devastated. There was an inquiry about who should be held responsible for the accident. Local and national news stations flooded the tragedy with coverage, and the focus was on me. I was the villain.

I didn't think their consensus was unfair.

No criminal charges were brought against me. However, the operator was convicted of negligent homicide. My case was dropped, as the inquiry couldn't find evidence to show I was directly responsible.

Even though the courts absolved me of blame, I've never forgiven myself. Not only did I hurt those on the road, but I also inflicted pain on the people who cared for me most—my family.

My passion for technology undermined my judgment.

Chapter Eight

After receiving the call about the incident, I sobbed and drove for hours in no particular direction. Eventually, I stopped at a gas station and sat in the car until I had no more tears to shed. When I finally looked at my phone, I saw numerous missed calls and messages from my brother, my mother, and my then husband. They were frantically looking for me, but the most-recent text message, from my brother, shot a wave of terror into my chest:

> There was another accident. Call me ASAP.

My hands shook as I fumbled with my phone, trying to dial his number through a haze of fear.

"Where are you?" he shouted. I'd never heard his voice sound so urgent.

"Eli? Another accident? You mean the crashes I caused?"

"No, sis! Tell me where you are."

I immediately knew something terrible had happened —something that might be even worse than the crash.

Fresh tears streamed down my face. "Just tell me what's happened first," I pleaded.

"Are you driving?" he asked.

"I'm not driving!" I shouted, my voice rising to a hysterical pitch. "Tell me right now what happened, or I swear I'll drive another hundred miles away."

"Okay, okay! It's William."

My husband. William. A suffocating darkness descended upon my body.

"What happened?" I whispered. "What do you mean it's William?"

"He was driving all over, looking for you, and he lost control of his car and ran off the road. He's at the hospital, I'm sending the address and location."

"On my way."

I raced to the hospital, fearing the worst and feeling as if I were being pulled into an ever-deepening pit of darkness. I'd caused another crash. I'd caused more harm. William was the victim. He'd been searching for me, and it had led him to the hospital.

I ran through the hospital doors and my brother appeared from nowhere and took me to my husband. I almost didn't recognize him in the hospital bed, with his face swollen and most of his body covered in bandages.

Thinking he was unconscious, I felt my panic increasing, but a nurse quickly explained that he was sedated with strong pain medication. She then provided further details, explaining that he'd sustained fractures in his arms and rib cage—and that he was bleeding internally.

My college sweetheart, my first love. The man who'd stayed in the US to be with me, who followed his heart despite having to leave his family in the UK. The man I married in Las Vegas during the last year of our studies. It upset our families, but we couldn't bear to be separated.

I stayed at the hospital for two days, leaving my husband's side only when absolutely necessary. But just when I thought the worst had happened, things became worse. My father suffered a heart attack and passed away.

I'd tried to contact him the day before he passed away, and my mother had informed me he was sleeping. I'd found it odd that I hadn't heard from him throughout my time in the hospital, but my mother assured me that he'd been sick. His heart had surely failed under the strain of the accidents that his daughter caused.

With his passing, the ground beneath me crumbled. How much more could I endure before I fragmented into irreparable brokenness?

Through the sheer force of my love for William and my determination to help him recover, I persisted. I carried on with life as best as I could, grieving and crying whenever I had a moment to myself. After Dad's funeral, my mother and I stopped speaking. I could see it in her blame-filled eyes. It was all my fault.

William stayed in the hospital for over a month and made slow but promising progress. The first time he spoke, three weeks after the accident, he said, "I w-want to g-get back h-home."

I initially didn't understand him. He kept repeating it, growing increasingly agitated and prompting the doctor to administer a calming drug. As he relaxed into sleep, I watched his face—a usually charming face that now bore a pained expression and many scars. It wasn't the physical scars that alarmed me but the haunting emptiness in his eyes and the absence of his radiant smile.

When he woke up, he was calmer. I sat next to him on the bed and held his hand.

"You want to go home," I said.

He closed his eyes and gave the tiniest nod.

"We will, darling. You'll be discharged in a few weeks, and we'll go home."

"H-home. E-England."

My heart ached, but I smiled. "Of course we'll go home to England." It pained me that he didn't long to go back to our home in Boston, that it wasn't the sanctuary he sought.

When he was released from the hospital, we left the US and moved to Oxford, to be close to his family. I was able to leave the country without the inquiry necessitating my presence. I stayed home to care for William, and we tried to build the perfect family we'd both once dreamed of, but he continued to suffer from nerve damage, whiplash, and headaches.

William's long recovery changed him, and our college dreams of having two children, one girl and one boy, were never realized. I knew his parents couldn't forgive me, however much they tried to hide it, and I couldn't blame them. I also knew William still loved me, but he no longer looked at me with awe and admiration.

A year went by. And then one afternoon, he blurted, "I want a divorce."

For the first time since the accident, he looked me in the eye, deep and long. With every molecule of my being, I wanted to fight him, to fight for our marriage. Instead, I nodded, hiding my pain.

I'd failed to rescue him or our love. I needed to set him free.

The divorce happened quickly, and I moved to London.

Now here I am, renting a room. I learned my lesson. I now keep people and technology at arm's length and refrain from forming intimate connections. This way, I'll never again inflict any pain on anyone.

Chapter Nine

For the past two years, I've been making my way from the confined quarters of my bedroom in North London to various work offices by train. This morning on my commute, my thoughts are consumed by how I should broach the subject of the recording with Sarah.

After exiting the train, I walk to Pages and Beans in hopes of seeing the friendly barista.

"Good morning! The usual?" he asks, looking at me as if he knows me better than anyone.

I nod.

"I'm Roy," he adds.

"I'm Dasia. Nice to meet you."

During my few minutes in the café, I imagine myself happy, healthy, successful, and in love. None of my past mistakes and hurts exist at Pages and Beans Café.

Hearing the recording yesterday shook me to my core.

I'd thought CEOs like Mr. Goodwin were just fictional characters in TV dramas, but now I can see that they exist in the real world. I can't figure out what to make of Luke, though. I'm in a sea of confusion. Perhaps he's a calculating yes-man in disguise. But whenever I see Luke and Sarah together, it seems as if he genuinely cares for her. Does he have Oscar-worthy acting skills?

I step out of the elevator at 7:30 a.m. holding my cortado.

As usual this early in the morning, the office is quiet. I put my purse on my desk and see Sarah in her office. "Good morning," I say with a wave.

She steps out and walks over to my desk, holding a photo.

"Look at this, Dasia. My granddaughter is getting a science prize at her school. She designed a device for people with lost limbs. It's a box with a mirror, when the individuals arm moves within the device, it gives the missing arm to experience sensations." she says, pointing to the photo, "they can feel the missing limb. Isn't that wonderful?"

"That's awesome!" I exclaim.

"She even dedicated the award to me." Sarah's eyes light up as she basks in the warm glow of pride. "My granddaughter has a friend who lost her arm when she was a baby, and her friend told her that the missing arm still occasionally needs a scratch."

I look at Sarah with admiration. "Your granddaughter

has dedicated the prize to you because she wants to be as successful and caring as her g'ma."

With that, Sarah moves toward me and hugs me tight. I wonder if this is what it feels like to be her granddaughter. When she walks back to her office, I see her skip between her steps. I turn my gaze to the river, which blurs as tears gather on my eyelashes. A longing fills me. I wish my mother were proud of me. I hastily blink a few times then wipe the corners of my eyes.

Though I've known Sarah only a short time, I feel connected to her and care about her. However, I can't help but feel that I'm treading on thin ice. The clandestine conversation between Mr. Goodwin and Luke is running through my mind. I don't need any more secrets in my life.

With the end of my four-week contract rapidly approaching, I know I should tell Sarah what I heard. But I don't want to spoil her happiness today. And I can't stop thinking about how I might be able to help her.

Just before noon, Sarah's voice makes me jump.

"What are you lost in thought about?" she asks, compassion in her tone.

"Nothing, some silly thoughts."

"Can we have a chat, please?"

"Sure." I follow her into her office and sit in the chair in front of her desk.

She studies me for a beat. "I just had a meeting with Mr. Goodwin. The board agreed that I'll lead the automation project to improve things at the South London

Outpatient Hospital. You know about the troubles it's facing, right?"

I nod.

She leans forward, her arms on her desk, and laces her fingers together. "Even if there's only a very small chance of saving jobs, I'll try anything." She exudes calm and focus. Then a smile spreads across her face. "Dasia, you're a gem to have as an assistant. I appreciate all the new things you've introduced into my work in such a short time."

I've helped Sarah automate and organize some of her more cumbersome tasks.

"Just doing my job."

Sarah tucks her beautiful ash-colored hair behind her ear. "A good leader recognizes good work and finds opportunities to show appreciation. I appreciate you, Dasia."

"Thank you." I feel my cheeks reddening.

She studies me again. "You don't have family in London, do you? Let's exchange phone numbers. I'd love to stay in touch after you move on from here."

"Uh . . . okay. I rarely use my phone. But here it is."

I give her my number then add Sarah, and now she's the third contact in my phone, along with my brother and the temp agency. I wish I could stay to help Sarah, but I just can't risk staying on longer. I can't risk anyone finding out my secret.

I sigh when I emerge from Sarah's office. A searing pressure builds in my head. I'm overwhelmed with thoughts. Sarah now leads the automation project; Mr. Goodwin persuaded the board, but he doesn't believe in the project or Sarah. Luke is aware of all this, yet as far as I know, he's choosing to do nothing about it.

I rush to Pages and Beans for lunch, hoping to outrun my thoughts. Roy isn't there, but I ignore my disappointment. I order another cortado and a sandwich and head to the reading corner. The two wooden signs hang on the sides of the bookshelf, bringing a smile to my face:

"Books are a uniquely portable magic." ~ *Stephen King*

"I see books, I see coffee, I see a good day ahead." ~ *Unknown*

I take a seat in the dark-blue velvet armchair across from a pretty woman. Opening my book, I imagine the chair's wooden legs spinning and transporting me into a magical world.

As I read, my mind wanders and crafts a dreamlike narrative. In this tale, I'm the star. I'm seated at an elegant café, reading my book, when a handsome man's voice interrupts me.

"Shall we dance?"

He's familiar, with kind eyes. I take his hand, and we waltz across the London sky.

"Are you enjoying it?" he asks.

"Yes," I say. I suddenly grip my coffee harder and

almost drop it. Roy is standing next to me, a smile on his face. Was it Roy or the dream guy who asked me the question?

"You looked like you were a million miles away."

"Just savoring the coffee" is all I can muster.

Oh, how little you know, Roy.

I make a mental note to stop dreaming of silly dances over London.

As Roy returns to the busy counter, I realize that the daydream was the first I've had since the accidents. What caused the shift?

Back at the office, just as I'm settling into work, a familiar voice startles me.

"Is that a good read?" Luke's looking at the book on my desk—*To Kill a Mockingbird.*

Oh great, just what I needed to brighten my day. He stands there looking as captivating as a sunset. I guess I'll have to suffer the view.

I touch my hair—it's like my personal security blanket. When happy or anxious, I can't resist the urge to run my fingertips through my hair. I inherited its color from my father, who has Mediterranean heritage. It contrasts my light skin, which I inherited from my mother, my maternal ancestors are from Northern Europe.

"Do you like it?" he asks.

"My hair?" I respond, confused.

He chuckles. "The book."

"Ah, the book." I reach for it. "Harper Lee. Here, you have a look."

He takes it and flips through the pages, stopping at my bookmark. He studies the page. Finally, he locks his gaze on me.

"So you're into modern classics." He resumes flipping the pages.

"I'm into the moral nature of human beings, treating others with kindness."

He seems taken aback by my remark. "Have you ever thought of writing a book?"

Now I'm the one taken aback. "I don't think I could."

"I believe everyone has a story waiting to be told."

I look at him quizzically.

He drops the book on my desk. "This is one of my favorites," he says, before turning and walking away with long strides.

So we have one thing in common. Otherwise, we're a world apart. I touch the book's cover. Though I'm glad that I refused to join his impromptu book club, I can't help but think about what he said about everyone having a story.

"What was that about?" Charlene asks, as she returns to her desk. She doesn't wait for me to answer. She's one of those people who thinks having a good conversation means providing a full-on monologue. "What was he holding? A book? He looked deep in thought. Let me see it."

I hand the book to her.

"I wish I could read him like a book." She winks at me.

I smile and return to my numbers, metrics, and graphs. I'm creating an automated template for Sarah. I've also decided that before I leave, I'll develop a checklist to help her with the automation project.

"It's been weeks, Dasia, and I still don't know anything about your love life," says Charlene.

"What? I don't have a love life."

"What are the top three things you typically go for? Do you have a checklist?" She chuckles. "C'mon! Tell me?"

Of course I have a checklist. I have a checklist for everything. But I have no desire to share it with Charlene. And so, she heads off to another desk to pester someone else.

Not that I have any intention of dating, being an *avid reader* would undoubtedly be at the top of my list. I glance at the book on my desk and shiver as if a cold breeze is brushing my skin.

Chapter Ten

That afternoon, Sarah asks me for assistance with her computer. I promptly head to her office, ready to help her unfreeze her documents and reboot her system. Supporting and troubleshooting tech issues for Sarah is one of my favorite activities at work. It brings me great joy to share useful computer shortcuts with her, especially because she's so eager to learn.

The sinister voice of Mr. Goodwin creeps into my mind as I help Sarah. *"She's a long shot!"*

Inwardly, I respond, *I don't think so*, firmly rejecting his doubts.

Seated in her chair, I find myself the focal point of Sarah's attention. "You know, I loved my previous role as a director of operations. I spent a lot of time at the hospitals, working closely with the frontline teams." She gives a little sigh. "It was a big leap into uncharted territory, joining an executive team comprised entirely of men, but I embraced it. Taking a leap of faith can be daunting, but our true potential often lies outside the confines of our comfort zone. So here I am, the executive leader." She smiles. "I hope I can continue making a difference and also inspire my granddaughters. And I want you to know you've made the transition so much easier, Dasia—thank you."

The thought of Sarah depending on me makes my heart glow. But uneasiness also creeps into my chest. I can't help but wonder why. Maybe I'm not used to receiving appreciation, or perhaps I'm becoming emotionally attached to Sarah. Is her caring nature triggering the void left by my mother?

Then she poses the question I've been hoping she wouldn't ask.

"I know your contract is ending next week, but would you consider staying as a project assistant for six months?" she asks, with a hopeful voice. When I hesitate, she adds, "Are you willing to leap, Dasia?"

People like Sarah can leap toward their potential. But people like me must jump away from their potential to avoid hurting people. I'm happy that I've built a life far from my potential.

I fix my gaze on the desk. "Sometimes when you leap, you only see your world turning upside down." Painful memories rush to my mind, yet Sarah's eyes light up.

"But if it's upside down, maybe you can see its depths more easily." She graces me with a radiant smile. "And sometimes you leap and discover that a bridge appears beneath your feet with someone named Dasia walking toward you."

I exhale.

I understand what she's saying, but I have no desire to turn my life on its head and examine it. No matter how flattered I am by her request, I can't stay. I have to leave next week. Suddenly, Sarah gasps. She's looking at her computer. I peek at her screen.

```
Sarah,
We have a problem; come to my
office.
A
```

I clench my teeth.

Noticing my expression, Sarah clears her throat. "Don't worry. He enjoys ordering people around, especially women, but I know how to handle him."

She sweeps confidently out the door.

On her way back from the meeting with Mr. Goodwin, Sarah stops in front of my desk. "Let's continue our chat."

Swallowing, I grab my electronic notepad and follow Sarah into her office.

A deep breath escapes her lips. "We're in a dire situation, Dasia, but all our analyses indicate that we may be able to prevent layoffs with the digital automation project. Implementing more efficient processes will significantly reduce costs." Her eyes are sharp and determined. "I really hope you'll stay."

"I don't know how to support a project like this," I blurt. My words continue tumbling out rapidly. "I don't think I'm the right project assistant. I don't have the skills to help you with something this crucial."

Sarah leans back in her chair. "I've seen your potential, Dasia."

I bite my bottom lip.

"You'd continue working closely with Luke and me. Not too much change."

I need to disclose the possibility of her job being at stake. It's a now-or-never moment.

"Sarah, I heard Mr. Goodwin talking about job losses. He doesn't believe in the automation project." I inhale and add, "You might even lose your job."

For a moment, I'm terrified. How will she take the news?

But to my surprise, she looks unfazed. "I know, Dasia. I'm taking a big risk here. But I believe the automation project will make a difference. I've analyzed the numbers for days. There's a chance we can save these jobs, so I'm going with it."

I blink. She's calm—and she also doesn't seem curious about how I overheard Mr. Goodwin's conversation.

Her phone rings, and she swiftly reaches for it. "You'll at least consider it, won't you?" she asks.

I simply nod in response.

I think of the tough road ahead of her. Sarah trusts me when I shouldn't be trusted. She sees me even though I'm a nobody. And she gives me encouragement and hugs that crack open the cold darkness in the depths of my soul.

During my commute home and while I'm cooking dinner, a heavy feeling sits on my throat, as if there's a large bag of cement on it. Nothing helps—not deep breathing, listening to calming music, or even reading a book.

I go to bed early and wish for sleep.

After I've finally drifted off, I jolt awake drenched in sweat, my heart beating in terror. In my dream, I was reading a newspaper with a disturbing headline:

"DASIA A. HARRIS COULD HAVE HELPED, BUT SHE DIDN'T."

Around me, in the dreamscape, Sarah and many other people, their faces contorted in agony, screamed into the darkness.

Another article bore this headline:

"MR. LUKE FERNSBY WINS THE YOUNGEST EXECUTIVE LEADER AWARD."

Below the headline is a photo of Luke drinking a celebratory cocktail with a pretty woman.

I sit up and try to shake off the horrific nightmare, my gaze darting around the dimly lit bedroom.

What is this darkness that pervades life, that brings injustice and unfairness? Must it always be this way?

I get up and open my laptop.

Hey Eli!

Remember how I always complained about life being unfair? Dad would say, "Sometimes, life won't be what we want, kiddo, but that's no reason to give up."

Have you ever considered how Mom felt about it all? I used to try to get her to see the injustice of her favoritism, but it was useless.

Do you ever think about how differently she treated the two of us?

Rather than hit the send button, I save this email as a draft. There are many more emails like this that I'm saving to share with my brother at a later date. I'm not quite brave enough to send them to him yet.

Chapter Eleven

After a mostly sleepless weekend, I arrive at work on Monday hoping to get through the week without any drama. As I start my computer, I hear Sarah's voice as she exits the elevator. She comes to my desk and makes herself comfortable in the chair opposite.

"Good morning. I hope you made up your mind and it's a yes."

I can't stay, yet my heart clenches when I think of people losing their jobs. If there's anything I can do to help, I should.

Then I think of Luke's face. Admittedly, it's a handsome face, but what good is a handsome face when he's happy to do Mr. Goodwin's bidding and doesn't care about anyone else? How can I work with him for another six months?

Sarah fiddles with my red stapler. "I know you must be worried about the project, but Luke will support it."

"Gee," I mutter, under my breath. "He's a godsend."

Sarah looks puzzled. "What did you say?"

"Oh, it's nothing."

As if summoned, Luke appears out of nowhere and greets us. He drops a few folders on my desk before turning his attention to Sarah. "I have a few potentials for the project-assistant position. Let's review them today."

Sarah turns and looks at me with pleading eyes.

Hot blood rushes to my head as I stare at the folders. How dare he. I haven't made an official decision yet. Is this a sign that he doesn't want Sarah to have a supportive project assistant? That he wants her to fail?

Before I know it, I hear words escaping my mouth. "I was just about to inform Sarah that I'll stay and take the position."

Abruptly, a chilling sensation spreads through my veins. I struggle to comprehend how my brain, heart, and lips have conspired against my will to do what I know is best for me.

Sarah stands and rushes toward me with open arms. Her hug almost knocks me out of my chair. Hugging her back, I see a tiny smirk on Luke's face.

What's that about?

Monday passes in a blur. I leave a pleased Sarah at work, yet an anxious knot tightens in my stomach as I start my journey home. My fear builds. I've taken a considerable risk. I wish I could slow the pounding in my chest.

I sometimes wonder whether humans must endure unpleasant encounters and memories indefinitely. Could I reshape my thoughts and mend my troubled mind? What if the human brain works similarly to a computer program, with every experience and memory we collect essentially coding our minds? If I were to flip the script, so to speak, and replace my mental zeros with ones, I could reprogram my brain and voila! All my fears would be gone. Then I could help Sarah.

I walk along the dark street lit by Christmas lights, on my way to an evening alone in my room. It's no surprise that Londoners begin decorating months in advance, given the shorter daylight hours leading up to the holiday. The bright lights appear in the shop windows in October, spreading hope, happiness, and joy.

At the Underground station, I find an empty seat on the train and pull out my book. I smile at a young girl sitting opposite me people-watching with wide eyes. She smiles back. I open my book, preparing to be whisked away to far-off lands filled with wonder and possibilities.

"Is that a romance book?" I hear his voice and feel the lines in the middle of my forehead deepen. This cannot be happening. But, oh yes, it's totally happening because he plonks himself right down in the seat next to me.

I ignore his question. "I didn't know you take this train."

"I'm going to a friend's house in North London." He's still eying the book in my hand. "I was surprised you decided to stay on. I thought you had much more exciting plans out in the world."

I keep a composed face. "I'm delaying my exciting plans out in the world for six months." I continue the sentence in my head. *So I can help Sarah and all the others you chose not to.*

I'm convinced he heard my silent sentence. He stares into my eyes and says, "I'm actually pleased you're staying." I want to believe him, but I don't.

He tilts his head a little. "Let's start again."

"Start what?"

"Start as if it's your first day at work."

I play with the ends of my hair. I have no idea where he's going with this.

He flashes a smile, one I can't help but find alluring, despite how I feel about him.

"I see a team of winners here. If we work together, I know we can conquer any challenge, whether it's climbing the highest peak or crossing the vast ocean." His nostrils flare like a dragon's.

"And which ocean are you referring to?" I ask. I wish I could hose his smile down with a vast stream of ocean water.

"Well, any ocean will do, I suppose," he replies, with a puzzled expression.

I force a grin. "I'd prefer to know which ocean we're talking about."

His smile fades. "Metaphorically, Dasia. I'm referring to a metaphorical ocean."

"Even metaphorically, I prefer to know." I look back at my book. "I also need to know why we'd cross that particular ocean and, most importantly, who else is with us."

He sighs and looks away, but out of the corner of my eye I see him roll his eyes and smile slightly.

I won't climb any mountains or cross any ocean unless Sarah is with us. Meanwhile, Luke's already constructing a boat to cross the ocean without her.

"This is my stop," he says. "See you tomorrow."

With gritted teeth, I reply, "See you tomorrow." I'm furious with him, but no matter how much I dislike him right now, I have to stay so that I can help Sarah.

Chapter Twelve

Who am I to help? I can't stay! What in the world was I thinking? Where was my brain when I said that? How can I stick around for another six months? Am I being reckless?

I'm cutting carrots, and the crunching sounds aren't the answers I'm looking for. Each question makes the invisible hand around my throat squeeze tighter. I have tell Sarah that I've made a huge mistake.

When I arrived home, my stomach was churning like a washing machine, and as soon as I got to my room, I fell to my knees, placed my head in my arms, and let the tears stream out of my eyes. I don't know how long I stayed like that. Finally, I got up, washed up my face, changed into comfortable clothes, and walked into the kitchen.

Usually, cooking calms me; I feel better in the kitchen. I'm making a stir-fry with vegetables of all colors, a bright contrast to the overcast gray sky we've had for weeks.

A sharp pain shoots from my index finger into my hand.

Uh-oh.

Blood spreads over the knife, the carrots, and the counter. I lunge to get a sheet of paper towel to stop the bleeding. After applying some pressure, I inspect my finger. I cut it pretty deep.

"What have I done?"

Reapplying the pressure, I grab a piece of paper and a pen and start a pros and cons list.

PROS:
- Helping Sarah
- Mitigating job losses: Maybe?
- Financial stability: I need the money to afford this expensive city, with huge electricity bills
- Job continuity for a few months
- Giving myself a break
- Time at Pages and Beans
- Luke

I take a long look at my list and try to figure out why Luke is on it. I hurriedly scratched out his name from the pros side and add it to the cons instead.

CONS:
- Luke
- Working closely with technology

The number one con on my list is Luke. How can I keep a positive mindset when working with someone who has an agenda that could damage Sarah and others? A feeling of apprehension spreads over me, as if his face is staring at me from the list, persuading me that he shouldn't be listed as a con item.

Helping Sarah will give me purpose. Moreover, staying in this job will help me maintain financial stability. The uncertainty that accompanies gaps between contracts often leaves me anxious. What happens if I struggle to get another temporary job and need to share a place with more than two people? A former coworker lived in a six-person household. I have no desire to see what that's like.

Alternatively, I could consider returning to the States, make amends with my mother and joining the family business, as my mother long urged me to do. I visualize living in our massive family house with a grand bedroom, a walk-in closet, and a sprawling backyard, where I'd sip my morning coffee. I know my mother has kept my bedroom as I left it. I'd never have to worry about an electricity bill again.

But to my surprise, I realize that I prefer my small and humble bedroom here over the one I had back in New Jersey. What in the world is happening to me?

Rain drums on my window, urging me to decide. My cut finger becomes an unwitting participant, throbbing persistently despite having stopped to bleed. I grab my raincoat and step out for a walk. A walk always eases my mind, whatever the weather. As I stroll through the rain, my mind settles and connects with my heart.

I accelerate as though preparing for a jump—the leap. Although a chill runs down my spine again, the adrenaline rush sends a smile to my face. I can't help but wonder what the landing might bring. For now, I concentrate on putting one foot in front of the other while repeating to myself, *Take the leap and conquer your fears! Take the leap, and the net will appear! Take the damn leap!*

Tuesday morning, I wake to a dark, chilly winter day. It wasn't my alarm that woke me but the howling wind. I feel oddly buoyant listening to it. I pull the duvet over my head. Shortly after, my alarm goes off.

When I step out into the ghastly wind, my hair dances in all directions. I think about how for so long, my life has had only one season. No spring, summer, or even fall. Just winter.

I rush to the train and then scurry through the cold to Pages and Beans.

As I walk inside, I light up like a firefly when I see Roy's smile.

"Good morning, Dasia. How are you this morning?"

I have an overwhelming urge to tell him about my morning, my weekend, the day ahead, even the weeks coming. There's something about him that makes me want to tell him everything.

"I'm good, thank you," I say, feeling his coffee-brown eyes pierce through me.

He looks at my bandaged hand, and his brow furrows. "What happened?"

"Just a kitchen accident," I say, touching the bandage. "It's okay now."

"Oh good." I order my usual, and as he makes it, he says, "So I've been wanting to tell you something—I'm cycling for a children's charity and I'd love for you to come and cheer us on. Other customers will be there."

He hands me a leaflet. The event is called Ride for Smiles and Bags of Hope, and it supports children in foster care.

"It's not for some time," he continues, "but we plan months ahead, so we can get permits and raise donations. I really hope you'll be around."

I notice the emphasis on the word *really*.

"Sounds awesome," I say with a smile, grabbing my cortado. "I'll be around."

It's been a long time since I committed to future plans. Going from living week-to-week to suddenly saying "I'll be there" regarding an event a long time away feels strange. But warmth floods me—I'm unsure if it's related to Roy or the cycling event.

When I get to my desk, I'm still looking at the leaflet,

still smiling. Suddenly, the stars in my eyes fade. Luke is at the end of the corridor chatting with a female colleague. They burst into laughter.

Sarah's door is open, and she's standing by the window looking out, seemingly deep in thought. When she turns and sees me, a smile broadens on her face. She beckons me in.

"Good morning, Dasia. I can't express just how happy I am that you've decided to stay."

I smile but feel as if I'm on the edge of a cliff. A single misstep could lead to my doom—and perhaps the doom of others.

"Oh, Dasia, what's happened to your hand?"

"Just a cooking accident."

"Are you in pain? Take the day off if you need to."

"No need, but thank you, Sarah."

Despite the edge-of-a-cliff feeling, my heart and mind are finally in sync. Sarah can rely on me. I'm choosing Sarah over my fears. I have a long list of reasons to be terrified, but I'm determined to persevere.

What defines us in life are the choices we make, I think, as I leave her office with my chin up. It's something my father used to say. I've chosen fairness and helping others. I'm proud that I'm no longer cowering in fear.

As I replace my tennis shoes with a pair more appropriate for the office, Luke approaches and sits on the chair opposite my desk. I force a smile.

"Dasia."

"Luke."

He places his elbows on my desk and leans forward. "What happened to your hand?"

I shrug. "Cooking accident when I was preparing dinner."

"Was that dinner for one?"

I give him a none-of-your-business type of stare.

Without taking his eyes off my hand, he adds, "Maybe I should take you out for dinner this week, so you don't have to cook and use your hand."

I cringe a little but hope that he doesn't notice. I don't go out for dinner with people, especially not with a boss. He has that silly smile on his face again. Some might find it charming, but I see right through it.

I tilt my head and look at my computer screen. "Thanks for the consideration. I'm fine."

"All right," he says, as he stands, tucking a hand casually in his pocket. I watch him meander away.

Then I notice the smile on my face. I'm taken aback, realizing I'm flattered. My mind switches gears with lightning speed, and I find myself whispering to the empty corridor, "Not in a million years."

Hey Eli,

I've accepted a six-month contract with my current company. I know, it's against my recent policy. But I decided to take the risk because I have an opportunity to possibly help people keep their jobs. And my heart tells me to help Sarah, my boss. If there's even the tiniest chance I can make a difference, I have to try.

You'd like Sarah. She's the only female executive member, and the oldest member of the executive team. But she's not treated fairly—I don't think the new CEO likes her.

One of the company's hospitals is in a financial crisis, and Sarah is leading a digital automation project to turn around the figures. Yeah, you heard me. Digital automation. But I'll stay away from the tech side, as no one knows about my past.

The timing works well because my current contract ends during the Christmas period, when it could be difficult to secure another contract. I'll be the project assistant for the digital automation project. I can hear my heart beat whenever I say the title out loud. I'll be trusted and relied on.

I plan to be very careful. I'll help Sarah with day-to-day tasks and won't get into the software aspect. I'll not make another mistake. I won't hurt anyone.

It's dark outside, and my computer screen is the only light in my small room. The chill here adds to my anxiety about the coming days.

"Come back, sister," you might be saying. But don't worry, Eli. I plan to maintain my distance from my colleagues, and at the end of my contract, I'll return to my usual life, with shorter contracts and no connections.

Chapter Thirteen

With project related tasks, my job already feels different, although my new position doesn't start until next week. I'm in Sarah's office, creating a road map for the automation project, when Luke barges in.

Sarah and I stare at him as he drops some files on Sarah's desk. "I need to walk and clear my head." With that, he rushes out.

I bet he does, I think, but remain silent.

Sarah notices my expression. "You'll get used to him. He's a lovely guy. Give him time."

If you only knew, Sarah!

She continues. "He was only seventeen when he started working here." I'm surprised to find that I want to know more. "He was helping his elderly neighbor back in Bristol. Then he joined one of the hospitals as a care assistant."

I find it hard to imagine Luke caring for an elderly neighbor. It's hard to reconcile this with the fact that he's in cahoots with Mr. Goodwin and keeping Sarah in the dark.

"He's never wavered in his pursuit of climbing the ladder, no matter how difficult the climb. Of course, it's not an easy path from entry level to executive leader. But when I met him, he was an ambitious junior manager who wanted to improve things. And he did. He strategized and led most of our improvement projects, which benefited patients and staff."

My eyebrows rise. "Did he?"

"Yes. His innovative strategies helped this hospital group come a long way."

Huh. Luke, the passionate changemaker, apparently.

"How did you get your start here?"

"Ever since I was a child, I dreamed of becoming a nurse, and thankfully my parents supported my aspirations. I worked as a nurse for several years, then became a team leader and manager. And now, here I am in an executive role."

I smile. "That's wonderful to hear."

"But women have more to navigate than men, both professionally and personally, and I've had my share. I'll tell you all about it another time."

Back at my desk later, I can't help but think about my own past.

One weekend when I was eighteen and in my first year of college, I drove home for a visit. My hands ached because I was gripping the steering wheel so tightly. My knuckles were white and my palms sweaty when I parked in the driveway of my family's home in the affluent, suburban part of Mahwah, New Jersey, where my mom's parents and grandparents also lived.

I nervously walked in and found my mother standing tall in the kitchen in a perfect outfit, looking radiant. She walked toward me, and the distance between us felt like miles. Then, without a smile, she reached forward with her right arm and gave me a half-hug. What was with those half-hugs?

She started making small talk, asking me about my trip. Then she said abruptly, "Your father is becoming the CEO soon."

I set down my luggage. "That's great."

My mother studied me. "When your brother takes over, you'll be his right hand."

I smiled. *Sure, my degree from one of the world's best computer-science colleges will help me transform into a right hand. Then, I can develop software for you to operate the hand remotely.* "Where's Dad?"

She pointed to his study.

I rushed over, knocked on the door, and entered. As soon as I reached him, he enveloped me in a hug.

"Are you going to be the CEO, Dad?"

"Yes, my petal, it's time." He looked sad. I didn't ask any more questions.

My mother was an only child and had inherited the

successful business from her third-generation Dutch American parents.

"Shall we take a walk, Dad? I've got a lot to tell you."

"I'm tired, sweetheart. I had a tough day."

I blinked in surprise. I'd never heard him say that before. He loved our walks.

My thoughts return to the present, and I think about those who may lose their jobs at South London Outpatient Hospital. Their lives may change drastically, as my father's did.

Shifting my attention back to the automation-project road map, I feel a burst of intensity. Questions claw at my mind: *Will it be enough? Can we prevent job cuts? Will this effort avert the crushing of hopes and dreams? How significant am I?*

Chapter Fourteen

O n the first day of my six-month contract, I step out of the elevator and head for my desk then quickly remember that I no longer sit next to Sarah's office. I turn and walk toward my new desk, in the project-team office. It's on the other side of the building and 123 steps from Sarah's office. The kitchen and my coffee maker are also farther away now. As is Charlene. I want to say that I'll miss her, but nope, that's not happening.

It might be easier to pop into Pages and Beans for my afternoon coffees. The thought makes me smile. But I won't see Roy this week. He's on his Christmas break. He told me that he always spends the whole Christmas week with his mother.

I'm grateful that Christmas will soon be over. We can all return to our normal lives.

I look around and see two team members quietly

talking at one of the desks. There will be four of us in the office, brought together for six months. Everyone else has already placed photos and other personal items on their desks; mine will remain unadorned.

I miss seeing Sarah's warm smile first thing in the morning, so I head toward her office. My heels count the steps with sharp *click-clacks*.

"Good morning," I say, popping my head into Sarah's office.

"Good morning, Dasia. I was just coming to see you. It's Christmas week!"

"Yes, it is."

"Come in." She beckons, and I step inside. "What are your plans for Christmas Day?"

"I plan to have a quiet Christmas, rest and watch TV."

Sarah shakes her head. "You're joining us for Christmas dinner at my house," she commands.

"Thank you, but I'm okay being at home. Also, don't you live outside London? I don't have a car."

"I'll take care of that. Edgar will pick you up in the morning, and you'll stay the night."

"Who's Edgar?" I ask. "Your husband?"

"My husband's name is Wesley. Edgar is a close family friend."

"I don't want to impose. And Christmas is in six days, Sarah. I don't have presents for anyone."

"You'll only have to worry about the twins, and I've spare presents for you if you can't find anything in the next couple of days."

I hesitate. "Are you sure? It's your family celebration. And who would want to drive on Christmas Day to pick me up?"

"I'm certain, dear. Everyone will be happy to meet you. You'll meet my husband, daughter, son-in-law, and fabulous granddaughters. And Edgar, of course."

"Sure, thank you, Sarah," I reply, taken aback by the sudden rush of excitement that courses through my body.

That evening, I step out of the office building feeling optimistic after the first day in my new role, at my new desk, in my new world. I even have an invitation to a family Christmas dinner. It'll be my first time buying Christmas presents in years.

I feel a spark in my chest; London seems to be winking at me through the festive decorations. I rush to Oxford Street to purchase some last-minute Christmas presents. As I dart in and out of shops, I feel happy to be with other shoppers. I feel a sense of belonging. I'm part of the crowd.

A guy with a thick beard holds a bunch of designer candles. He sniffs each one intently before finally settling on a pine-scented one. Two women have an intense conversation about a pair of fluffy slippers. As I turn a corner, I can't help but laugh at the sight of a young man with a pretty necklace around his neck looking utterly confused. He seems to be deciding whether to buy it.

I can't resist. "That necklace really brings out your eyes," I tease. A big grin spreads on his face.

A woman is considering an e-book reader for her father-in-law.

A woman buys a pretty bag for her daughter.

I'm in London shopping for Christmas presents for two girls I've never met. My excitement increases. I suddenly feel at home.

On Christmas Day, I wake up in an empty apartment. My roommates are spending Christmas with their families. In the shower, I start humming. Then I belt out the song I've been hearing everywhere for the last few weeks.

"It's beginning to look a lot like Christmas!"

Sarah told me to be ready by 11:00 a.m. and that it'd take around an hour to reach her home in Hertfordshire, north of London. She calls it "the manor," so I'm assuming it's a large house.

I hear the doorbell precisely at eleven. Just before leaving my small bedroom, I glance in the mirror one last time. Then I grab the bag with presents and rush downstairs feeling as if I'm about to step into a glittery, magical world. I open the front door and there stands an older gentleman with a huge smile.

"Merry Christmas, love." He's wearing a Santa hat, but his gray beard would need to be much longer for him to look like Santa.

"You must be Edgar," I say. "Thank you for driving all the way, and Merry Christmas."

I'm surprised as he leads me to the back seat of a black car with a cream leather interior. "There's practically no traffic. We should reach Much Hadham in forty-five minutes," he says, while I step into the back seat.

I turn around and ask, "Would you mind if I sit next to you?", taking the courage from my funny Christmas sweater.

"Of course," he responds.

We set off, and within fifteen minutes, the scenery changes. "Much Hadham," I whisper. I admire the tranquil countryside of Hertfordshire, with its green landscapes and large fields. It's not a white Christmas but a pretty, colorful one. It's mostly a silent ride.

Edgar turns into a country lane surrounded by open fields, and we soon approach a big gate that opens slowly. I gulp at the sight of an enormous red-brick house. He pulls onto a large circular gravel drive with a yew circle at its center bordered by manicured box hedges. My mouth drops open.

"Is this Sarah's house?" I ask, breathing a little faster with nerves.

"Yes, love. We're here."

The three-story mansion has symmetrical windows with panes of glass separated by mullions, painted white to contrast the red brick. Nestled within the grand facade, two white columns grace each side of the red door, perfectly fitted into the expansive white frame. The mansard roof has atticlike windows. I'm dazzled.

Sarah rushes out smiling from ear to ear, her arms

open. *It's beginning to look a lot like Christmas*, a voice whispers.

She leads me to a large, comfortable seating area with a giant Christmas tree. The room is decorated from top to bottom with wreaths, garlands, and twinkling lights. As we approach, the activity in the room—children running and adults chattering—comes to a halt. All attention shifts to us.

"Everyone," Sarah announces, "meet Dasia."

"Welcome. I'm Wesley, Sarah's husband. It's a pleasure to have you here." He grips my hand firmly. He's wearing a festive pin and emanates both authority and warmth.

I'm then introduced to Sarah's daughter and son-in-law and to Isabella and Gabrielle, Sarah's twin granddaughters.

Sarah hugs Edgar. "See you tomorrow."

He'd told me during the drive that he'd be spending Christmas with his family.

"Edgar's been working for my husband's family since he was a teenager," Sarah said, once he's gone. "He's practically family."

I'm quiet as I take in my surroundings, feeling as if I've just walked into a Christmas wonderland.

The day passes in a blur of laughter, delicious food, games, and merriment. Throughout the celebration, as I watch Sarah and her family, I'm reminded that I'm also a daughter, a grandchild, and a sister.

After dinner, Sarah settles herself under the tree and picks up the presents one by one, shouting out names. We all watch each other excitedly unwrap the gifts, and I'm touched when she holds out a thin box and shouts my name.

As I take hold of my present, I'm filled with joy and a hint of embarrassment. All eyes are on me as I unwrap it, and the twins are excitedly giggling. It truly is a wonderful Christmas. Anticipation fills the room as I tear off the pretty wrapping paper, and I gasp when I see the voucher inside.

The voucher is a piece of art in itself, decorated with elaborate motifs and beautiful images that perfectly encapsulate the spirit of a traditional British afternoon tea. There's also a picture of a table set with elegant silverware, white linens, and an assortment of delicacies.

A famous hotel's name is printed on the voucher. What a gift—the promise of a lavish afternoon in a dazzling environment!

Then I notice that the certificate is good for two individuals. I squint at Sarah and tilt my head.

She grins.

I feel like a whole new person.

Chapter Fifteen

I n the first week of January, the holiday excitement is replaced with a different kind of excitement. I'm with my new team, and we're having a project meeting. These meetings are different from the ones I supported Sarah and Luke at previously. They're called huddles—instead of sitting around a conference table, we stand in a circle. The energy feels new and different.

Sarah explains, "We go round the circle, and everyone gets to have a say. No one interrupts until the round is completed."

Today, I'm also excited about what I have lined up for tonight. A few weeks ago, I scored a ticket for a jazz concert at Ronnie Scott's, in the heart of Soho. I can already imagine myself tapping my feet to the rhythmic beats and losing myself to the soulful melodies. And my roommate Jay is also coming. Although we've lived together for quite some time, we've only recently connected. Jay and I both like cooking.

A few weeks ago, we were both in the kitchen, and Jay said, "Why don't we cook for each other? Tonight, I'll make a dinner for both of us. Then another night, you can do the same. I'm always intrigued by your ingredients and dishes. And we can have a friendly chat." He looked at me with hopeful eyes. "It's a win-win, right?"

I froze a little. He noticed.

"Don't worry, I'm not trying to pick you up. You're a beautiful woman, but I'm not interested in dating you.

I looked at him as if I'd never seen him before.

He continued chopping his herbs. "To be honest, I desperately need to talk about my disastrous date last night. This drop-dead gorgeous man turned into an ugly frog. In return, I'll offer a delicious dinner. How about that?"

I grinned. "Fair enough."

And that was that. We now take turns cooking for each other two nights a week, and we have a little competition to see who can make the most delicious dinner.

I feel safe around Jay. He doesn't know my secret, and I have no reason to disclose it. Not yet, anyway.

Jay is laid-back and likes to talk, and I love his zest for life. He's tall, attractive, fit, and blessed with gorgeous olive skin from his Indian background. Whatever color he wears, he looks fantastic. He's also charming.

One night, he snatched my notebook and began writing

something. I was aghast, but it was impossible to be upset with him.

"What are you doing? Practicing your calligraphy?"

"I'm not practicing. Just easing your straight lines. Too many sharp corners. I can't breathe when I see them."

I frowned in confusion.

Minutes later, he turned the notebook to face me.

I gasped at the sight of my name written in the most elegant letters I'd ever seen. He'd positioned thin but graceful shadows behind some of the letters.

I ran my fingertips over the curls and lines of the seamlessly flowing letters.

"The shadows are as crucial as the light."

I met his gaze for a moment. His eyes were firmly fixed on me.

I tilted my head slightly and nodded, looking at my name again. I couldn't help but get lost in the beauty of the letters. He's a phenomenal calligraphy artist.

The next morning, I entered the kitchen and was greeted by his cheerful voice. "Hey there, Sparkles!"

"Sparkles?"

"Soon shalt thou uncover," he said with a wink.

"What?"

"You do not know, but soon you'll discover—your shine."

Even though our cooking evenings started only a few weeks ago, it feels as if Jay has been part of my life for much longer. We have contrasting personalities, but I find myself surprisingly at ease around him.

Over the holidays our other roommate moved out, and yesterday, I was enjoying the delicious meal that Jay cooked when he blurted, "How about we share the rent of the third room and request that the landlord not rent it to someone else? How about we start the year off with the gift of a living room?"

"You and me only, with a living room?"

He gave me an exaggerated nod and a broad grin.

"Why not? Let's do it!"

I have a living room. Life is good. And tonight, I'm going to listen to jazz.

I leave the office hurriedly, although I have plenty of time. I feel a rush of exhilaration as my legs propel me to the Underground.

I hop onto the train and search for an empty seat. When I find one and sit down, I catch sight of Luke in the distance. He doesn't see me, as he's absorbed in the evening paper. We both step off the train at my stop, near Soho, but he still doesn't see me. *I wonder why he took this train.*

As I walk to the jazz club, I realize that newfound joy is coming at me from all directions. Have I opened myself up to life again? Or have I simply stopped running away and allowed life to happen to me?

I take in the hustle and bustle of London on a Thursday evening. Everywhere there are people with cameras, immortalizing the moment. I'll be one of those people caught in the background, walking through the frame of another person's memory. I've already heard five different languages in five minutes, and I love that I'm a Londoner.

Jay is waiting for me at Ronnie Scott's. I'm overjoyed; I had to dip into my savings to get these tickets, and we'll be in the back row, but it doesn't matter.

While we wait for the show to begin, I glimpse a figure out of the corner of my eye. I do a double take. It's Luke. What in the world is he doing here? I watch in disbelief as he walks toward us, my mind racing.

"Hello, hello," he says.

I force a smile and introduce him to Jay.

Luke waves at someone, and moments later a gorgeous woman joins us. She and Luke hug and give each other kisses on the cheek. He introduces his date to us. She has dark wavy hair and well-defined cheekbones. Everything about her gives off an artsy vibe—the clothes, the eyeliner, the makeup.

"Dasia, shall we?" Jay's voice snaps me out of my trance, pulling my attention away from the captivating woman.

With a sense of urgency, we make our way to our seats, and soon, the music starts and fills all my senses.

At one point I notice Luke and his date at a dinner table in front of the stage; he also seems to be lost in the music.

When the concert ends, I grab my coat. "Let's get out of here fast to beat the crowd." Jay agrees, and we make our way to our Underground station. "A superb performance," I say. "It was dreamy."

"He's dishy, you know," Jay says. "And he wants you."

"Who?"

"You know who. Your boss."

"He so does not! Didn't you see the woman he was with?"

"Hard not to." Jay's playful tone catches me off guard, making me blush slightly. "I couldn't help but notice how closely you were scanning her."

"I wasn't scanning—I was simply appreciating her beauty," I retort.

Jay leans toward me and whispers, "By the way, I noticed him stealing glances in our direction. I think he might have mistaken me for your boyfriend. Talk about adding fuel to the fire!"

"Hardy har har, Jay."

A tiny smile forms on my lips before I realize what I'm doing. I promptly wipe it away.

Chapter Sixteen

In my bedroom, I still feel the effects of the jazz. It's as if happy energy is lingering in the air. It's a strange feeling for me, happiness.

From an early age, all I wanted was my mother's approval. I thought that was the key to my happiness. But her approval was simply out of reach. And no matter how much praise I received from my father, brother, teachers, neighbors, and community, she never seemed to be satisfied. And I was unhappy.

The moments of happiness I've had these last few weeks have had nothing to do with my mother's approval —a cozy living room, a soulful jazz concert, the company of a dear friend, the charm of this vibrant city.

My gaze lands on the photo of my brother and me in front of our home. We were nine and ten years old, respectively. The image captures the moment when I sprayed him with a hose, soaking his clothes and hair. We loved playing with water. He's laughing, shielding his face with both hands. There's a small rainbow between us, created by the sun and the water droplets suspended in the air. I love this photo. It reminds me of how much I cherish our relationship and how much I miss him.

Though I might not have the life I desire, tonight, I'm choosing happiness.

I rummage through my drawer and select two face masks. Then, instead of staying in my bedroom as I usually do, I shout out, "Jay, let's put on some beautifying masks and watch a movie."

We apply the masks, and when I look at Jay, we burst into laughter.

My thoughts are aligned with the delight I feel.

I choose face masks. I choose lightness around my heart. I choose this moment.

Tonight, I choose happiness.

Chapter Seventeen

The automation project is progressing well. Today, Sarah is giving the project team a motivational Monday morning talk.

"We're all experts in our own areas, and we'll achieve success only if we work together. It's like being part of a rowing team—each person matters, but the team members' synergy makes or breaks the race."

I admire Sarah more each day. We all listen to her with respect and curiosity.

"We need to work together to make this project a success and save jobs," she says, while looking around the room.

Luke reclines in his chair, casually crossing his legs. "Dasia, as you're the master of metaphors, tell us what we need to do to cross an ocean as a team." He wears that little smirk.

I just smile and offer a playful retort of my own. "We

explore the best ways to cross it. The option that immediately comes to mind is swimming, but obviously, it's not the ideal solution. We need to think bigger. Find something that will get all of us safely to the other side."

"So, we need to build a ship?" Luke asks mischievously.

"It doesn't have to be a huge ship, but some vehicle that we can all board." I look pointedly at Luke, wanting him to understand that Sarah isn't alone.

"What sort of vehicle?"

So, this huddle will be a long one. I step to the flip chart. Its stand is armed with colorful markers. Once I'm there, my confidence falters, and I suddenly feel like a lost child in a sea of scribbles. But I steady my hand and start. Sure, I have the drawing abilities of a three-year-old, but I can rock some serious shapes and math.

"Sometimes all we need is a small boat. And everything we need to build one is already within us."

I begin by drawing a horizontal rectangle. Then, I draw a triangle on each end to make it a trapezoid, like a boat. Next, I draw a smaller vertical rectangle, which becomes the boat's mast. Finally, I add a triangle sail. Voila! I've created a magnificent boat that would make Picasso jealous.

The team breaks into a round of applause, and I bow and feel excitement shooting out of my eyes like tiny stars. Spotting Luke's heavy gaze, I feel my smile fade.

"Let this humble boat be our inspiration," Sarah says. "It's all about simplicity and unity. Each of us has a place on this boat, which can embark on a journey of endless possibilities."

I nod and add, "Once we're in the boat, the tide will raise all of us, or we'll all sink."

I look around at my teammates, unsure if Luke is with us or will sail on a different boat with Mr. Goodwin. But Sarah is radiant. She is the stroke of our rowing team, the one who sits at the back of the boat and sets the rhythm. To lead, sometimes you need to stay at the back.

After everyone has left, Luke remains in his chair and watches me while I gather the meeting notes.

"I didn't know you liked jazz." He raises his brow.

"I don't like jazz. I love jazz."

"I can see that."

Luke's eyes narrow, as if he's thinking of saying something else, but he doesn't. I remember how gorgeous his date was then quickly wave away the memory.

He glances at his computer screen, looking troubled. "We don't have the up-to-date visuals for the project website. I've uploaded them but can't see them. Bloody hell, I need them for my next meeting."

Just as he's about to call the IT department, I walk over.

"Let me look at it."

With a dazed expression, he stands and offers his chair. "All yours."

I access our project page. With a quick Command+comma, a few more strokes to flush the cache, and a reboot of the browser, we're back in business.

"Here they are. All the visuals are back now."

He's giving me that heavy stare again. I look at the screen to avoid it.

"Sarah told me you're excellent with computers."

I shift a little in the chair. "Yeah, I like them, but this was an easy fix." I can hear my heart whizzing like an overheated laptop.

"You also like maths and straight lines. There was no curve on your boat." A curious grin forms on his face.

"Well, our little boat is sailing through curvy waves. I'm not as straight-lined as you think." I shoot him a coy look and head for the door. Did I just bat my eyelashes?

"Believe me, I noticed that too."

Oh no, he's flirting—and a not-insignificant part of me likes it. But, walking away, I can't stop imagining him tumbling from Mr. Goodwin's yacht into huge waves while the rest of us watch from our simple boat.

A light dusting of snow covers London on Wednesday. It's pretty, but many project members can't get to work as they travel from a distance, and public transport isn't the most reliable in snowy London.

I'm busy with tasks when an email pings on my screen. It's from Luke.

Could you please help?

I reluctantly leave my comfortable desk and walk toward his office.

"Ah, Dasia, come in. We have an emergency board meeting tomorrow and need several critical documents from the archive department."

"Sure, I'll get there first thing in the morning."

"I'm afraid the meeting is early in the morning. We'll need these documents today to prepare."

"But the archive department isn't even in this building, and it's snowing," I say, in a tone that's almost a growl. It's almost 4:00 p.m., and daylight is fading fast.

Luke shrugs, raising his shoulders and flipping both palms up, and says sorry. I'd believe him if I didn't know him better. I snatch the list of documents from him and stalk out.

The archive department is in a building a mile south of our office. I decide to take a taxi, although this is an unwarranted expense. I haven't been to the archive building before and can only hope everything is in order so I can easily find the files.

When I step into the building I'm greeted by a friendly security guard.

"Hello, I'm Dasia, from the head office, here to access some files for Luke.

"I'm meant to be informed before your arrival, love," he says, looking confused. "But let me see if I have a notification from Luke." He clicks and clacks on his keyboard. "No, love, I don't have any request."

He calls Luke, who doesn't pick up. We make small

talk, and several minutes later he calls again. Thankfully, Luke answers this time.

"Hello, Luke, Harold here from the archive. I have a young lady here requesting access to some files." He listens for a moment. "Splendid," he says, and hangs up.

He gives me an access card and leads me to the elevator and then to a huge room with shelves and shelves of folders. He points out the letters, aisles, and numbers. I thank him for his kindness. He looks hesitant but leaves me.

I almost choke on the dust in the air, and I'm shocked at the sight of the many files piled messily on the shelves. I walk the aisles slowly and touch some folders.

We overload our brains precisely like this, I think. *How many folders are piled up in my brain, I wonder? Messy ones, sad ones, happy ones, hidden ones.*

Despite the mess, it doesn't take me long to locate four of the files Luke asked for, but I search and search for the final one. When I look at my watch, I see it's nearly 6:00 p.m.

Suddenly, there's a loud *thunk*, and then another.

I scream as the lights go out and darkness envelopes me like a thick blanket. I grip a shelf and tremble, looking around. It's pitch-black, as there are no windows.

I reach for my phone, remembering it has a powerful flashlight. I turn it on, and my breathing calms a little. Holding the four files tightly, I hurry toward the door.

Then, with a few more loud *thunks*, all the lights come back on in a blinding explosion.

I freeze and shrink. Once my eyes have adjusted, I see Harold coming out of the elevator. He rushes toward me. "I'm sorry, love. I turned off the lights by mistake. I hope I didn't scare you. Oh, dear, you look pale."

Adrenaline pumps through me, and I jump into the elevator as fast as a cheetah. Meanwhile, Harold moves like a giant tortoise. I try to be patient as I hold the door for him.

Dust clings to my clothes and hair as I leave with the four files. *The fifth one must be lost.*

When I get back to the office, it's empty. The silence is eerie. I push away my anxious thoughts. Assuming that Luke will return for the files this evening, I leave them on his desk with a note saying I couldn't find the fifth file.

When I arrive home, it's just before 9:00 p.m. I'm exhausted.

I start my commute earlier than usual and arrive at the office just before 7:30 a.m. Luke is in his office, his head buried in files.

I knock on his door. "Morning," I chirp.

"Morning," he responds distantly.

Did you expect him to give you a medal or something?

"I left the files on your desk, but I couldn't find the fifth folder. I searched for it for an hour."

"Okay." Then, not looking at me, he points at a file on

his desk, and my eyes pop out—it's the file I'd been looking for. He'd had it all along.

I cross my arms and glare at him. He doesn't notice initially. When I don't move, he finally looks up.

"Thank you," he says curtly.

I leave his office, annoyance flowing through my veins like lava. My mother often said "Okay" when I completed a challenging task and wanted her to see how hard I'd worked.

I march to the kitchen to get a glass of water and calm myself. Someone is already there when I arrive.

"Hey, Dasia."

I plaster a fake smile on my face. "Hi, Emilia."

"I'm glad that the automation project is going really well." She's leaning on the counter.

"Yes, it's going well," I say, filling a glass. I focus on the water. Emilia supports the project when needed from an HR point of view.

"Working for Luke must be fun," she says. I turn off the tap and look at Emilia. The fluorescent lights in the sterile office make her smokey eye makeup look overly done and out of place. "He's such a mystery when it comes to his dating life. Do you know if he's seeing anyone? I think maybe he's married to his work. He seems like one of those guys."

Curiosity spreads through my mind like wildfire. "I don't know," I say, which is true.

"Come on, Dasia. Promise you'll tell me if you find out anything."

I take a deep breath. "Sure," I say, and walk off, feeling her eyes burning holes in the back of my head.

Once I reach my desk, I drink the water, place the glass on my desk then stare at it. No matter how much we try, sometimes we can't keep the glass full.

Chapter Eighteen

Usually, time races by at the office, but today, each minute drags. When it's finally lunchtime, I remove the empty glass from my desk, open my drawer, and take out the leaflet Roy gave me.

I seize my purse and coat then swiftly make my way out of the building. I close my eyes for a beat and picture Roy asking me out on a date. A slight shiver runs through me, and I'm not sure what's caused it—standing outside on a cold, snowy January day without a scarf or thinking about Roy.

I can't help but smile when I enter Pages and Beans. It's buzzing with people chattering, ordering drinks, and eating lunch. My gaze darts around; I don't see Roy. My grip on my book gets tighter with anticipation as I order lunch, but he's nowhere to be seen. Finally, I settle at a small corner table by the wall, away from the book corner as the cute armchairs are occupied.

"Hey." Hearing his comforting voice, I look up. He stands next to me wearing a brown apron. His dark hair falls in waves, and his smile is wide and charming. "I was about to take my lunch break. Can I join you?"

"Of course. But will you be okay? The café seems very busy."

"Nah, it's fine. I'll just grab something to eat. Do you want anything else?"

"No, thanks." I smile.

This isn't a date! I repeat in my head a few times. He didn't ask me out. I was already here. We're simply two people on our lunch break.

I've just taken a bite of my sandwich when he returns without his apron and sits beside me. He exudes a relaxed yet confident vibe in his simple white T-shirt and dark jeans. He places a small plate of tarts on the table, and I notice his very slight belly. He must love the cute pastries here. I bet he doesn't spend hours at the gym.

"Those look yummy! And this sandwich is scrumptious."

"I'm chuffed you like it. It's my favorite on the menu too." He takes a bite of his sandwich and closes his eyes for a beat. "The arugula adds a nice peppery finish." He holds up the sandwich and looks at it as if it's a precious piece of jewelry.

"You're pretty passionate about a sandwich," I say, taking another bite.

"I'm passionate about everything we offer here. Food doesn't just nourish the body—it also nourishes the mind and soul. It's a source of pleasure and connection. Food brings people together, stimulates our senses, and tells stories of culture, history, and memories."

I stare at him in awe. "I wholeheartedly agree with every single word you just said." Then I ask, "How long have you worked here?"

"From day one. I own it."

My sandwich sticks in my throat, and I take a gulp of coffee to help it go down. "You own Pages and Beans Café?"

His eyes widen. "Didn't you know? Yeah, it's been a few years now."

"I'm sorry, I didn't know! It's a fantastic place," I add.

A glow of pride adorns his face. I feel good around him. Holding a conversation with him is easy. Or maybe the olive oil in this delicious sandwich is liquid courage.

"What did you do before?" I ask.

"I worked here and there in the corporate world, which didn't agree with me. Then I lost my sense of direction for a while. This place grounded me."

"Connecting with a place on such a deep level must be awesome." I say as he looks around in awe, nodding.

I take out the leaflet from my purse and gesture to the small map on it. "So where should I stand to cheer you on?"

He grins. "You're coming!"

"Yes, of course. I promised."

"I look forward to seeing your bright smile there."

A subtle warmth tingles in my cheeks. As he points out the optimal location to observe from, I lean closer to him. The scent of espresso wafts off him while we study the map, our heads mere inches apart.

"Good afternoon."

Luke's unexpected greeting interrupts our intense moment. He stands next to us, looking frustratingly charming, and stares with a look that suggests I'm a stranger. There's a moment of awkward silence.

Roy casts a swift glance at both of us before addressing Luke. "Afternoon, sir."

"Afternoon, Luke," I say. "I was just about to tell Roy that I've got to get back to the office."

A subtle frown crosses Roy's face as he glances at Luke again.

"Thanks for joining me, Roy."

"Pleasure is mine, Dasia. Anytime." He follows suit as I stand. Luke steps back to allow me to pass.

As I walk away from the table, I feel as if I'm stepping out of a Parisian café in a movie scene. Tiny green tendrils of spring spread into my heart in the midst of the winter day.

That afternoon, I make my way to Luke's office to meet with Sarah and him. The moment I step inside, my attention lands on the elusive fifth file, neatly placed on a small table. I'm both irritated and captivated by its presence.

As I settle in a chair at the table, Sarah walks in and takes a seat as well. She notices the unfriendly stare I'm giving the file and frowns in confusion.

"Luke," she says, "I never got a chance to thank you for saving me at the board meeting this morning."

"No worries, Sarah."

Then she looks at me. "Luke got the security team to open the archive department at 10 p.m. last night. He searched for that file"—she nods to the one on the table— "for over two hours until he found it."

I can feel my pupils expanding.

Sarah continues. "Then he turned up at 6:00 a.m. and helped me to prepare for the meeting. I couldn't have gotten the board's approval without his help."

I can feel his stare drilling into me with such intensity that I shift uncomfortably in my seat, trying to get away from it. But it's no use.

"Sometimes the truth lies just beyond what we can see, Dasia," he says with a grin.

I'd been wrong all along. He hadn't kept the file from me. He'd been helping Sarah. I can't help but wonder why.

Chapter Nineteen

The weeks go by quickly, but even as spring arrives, the early-March days remain chilly. Still, I catch sight of the occasional daffodil.

At work, we're running small implementation tests of the automation project. Earlier this morning, I left some reports on Luke's desk.

My phone rings.

"Can you spare a minute, please?" Luke asks.

"Sure, I'll be right over."

I make my way toward his office, pondering why he wants to speak with me. My high ponytail swings as my heels *click-clack* down the hall. With a deep inhale, I tap on his door.

"Come in, Dasia."

"How can I help?"

He's occupied with his computer. I can't help noticing

how his fitted shirt molds to his upper body. I glance at his screen and discover he's browsing for scarves.

"I need a favor, please. I'm trying to pick a birthday present. On my way home, I'll grab something from one of the shops downstairs. Which scarf would you choose?"

I love passing through the cute retail arcade, which has cafés, boutiques, and cake shops, on my way home. But it isn't the right place to buy a birthday present for someone special.

I press my lips together and crinkle them to one side. "Hmmm." I say, "Don't you like this woman?"

His eyes widen, and he tilts his head in astonishment. "Of course I do. These are expensive scarves."

"So you believe that an expensive scarf from the store next to your workplace has the power to make a woman feel as though she's soaring above the clouds, ascending higher and higher?"

He stares at me, confusion spreading across his face.

"I don't think so," I say, in answer to my question.

"What would take you above the clouds?"

"Well, it's not my birthday, and I don't want to be above the clouds, but let's see what we can do for your friend. First, tell me a bit about her." I find myself curious. I want to know more about his type.

"Well, she's your everyday kind of woman. She likes the simple things, like watching TV, cooking delicious meals, and enjoying the comfort of her own home."

His description takes me by surprise. His date at the jazz concert hadn't seemed like the type to derive pleasure from activities like that. I quickly remind myself not to be judgmental. *Appearances can be deceiving.*

"Hmm. How about planning an experience or a weekend trip? You can make it special, perhaps add champagne and flowers."

He leans forward. "What else?"

"If you want to stay home, cook her a romantic dinner and create a beautiful environment. Then, after the meal, mix her favorite drink and serve a personalized chocolate cake from a local bakery. Chocolate cake is the secret to success."

Luke gets up, puts both hands into his pockets, and walks to the window. He looks out, his back to me. His voice sounds different when he says, "What did you get from your boyfriend on your birthday?"

"We're talking about a birthday present to send your girlfriend over the clouds." *I hope she stays there and never returns to earth,* I hear my inner voice say. I feel a gentle blush color my face.

"It's for my mother," he replies, and as he turns around, all my negative impressions of him undergo an unexpected transformation. In that moment, I catch a glimpse of his sweet and caring side.

Moments pass, and I realize that I'm grinning—and that I haven't said anything since he told me the gift is for his mother. I need to stop staring at him and speak.

Say something. Say something.

"Okay, your mother. Of course." I swallow hard.

"We'll get something delivered on her birthday. When is her birthday?"

"Saturday."

"Next Saturday?"

"No, this Saturday, Dasia."

"But that's tomorrow, Luke."

"I know, Dasia."

"Gee, you're certainly on top of things."

"I know. I really need your help," he says, fluttering his eyelashes. "I'm usually better with this, but work has thrown me off-balance."

"Okay, let's get on it. Where does she live?"

"In Bristol, but she always comes to London and stays with me on her birthday."

Aw! I catch myself staring once more. *Say something, Dasia. Anything will do.*

I find my voice. "Well, that's easier. You can take her to a show or an event in London. I'm sure we can find something on very short notice." I stress the word *very.* "Hmmm. How about dinner and a show in Covent Garden?"

"She'd love that!" he exclaims. "Let me call my brother to see if he can join us. That would make her so happy."

He picks up his phone, and I listen to the short phone conversation that speaks volumes.

"Hey, mate, birthday show and meal tomorrow. Are you in? Yes, I'm planning. Okay."

For a moment, my thoughts drift to my brother and

how much I miss him.

"So, do we involve partners?" I ask, after he hangs up, thinking of his date at the jazz evening.

"Plans for three only."

I prepare to leave his office. "I'll work on it, but please don't leave it to the last second next time."

"I'll give you more of a heads-up next year." He grins, and I shoot him a sharp look.

"Thank you, Dasia. I owe you one."

"You owe me absolutely nothing. Happy to make a mother happy."

"Jay is a lucky guy," he says, as I leave. I smirk and continue walking out of his office, acting as if I hadn't heard what he said.

Back at my desk, I get to work planning a London evening. I immediately think of the Royal Circle at the Theatre Royal Drury Lane. And before the show, they can have a dinner nearby. I should have asked about his budget. He hadn't mentioned anything about that.

Sky's the limit! I think with a chuckle.

I slide into an imaginary world where I hear the laughter of my mother. My brother and I admire her; she looks back at us with loving, sparkling eyes. I thank the universe for the most wonderful mother, who loves her children equally. Then I blink a few times, getting back to reality. The fantasy was nice while it lasted.

Some people are luckier than others. Why else would my mother love my brother more than she loves me? Really, I'm not sure she even loves me at all. During my teenage years, I made a long list of reasons in an attempt to figure out why she treats me the way she does.

- *Am I the product of a love affair?*
- *Does she think I'm a witch?*
- *Is it because I'm a girl?*
- *Or maybe because I have silkier hair than she does?*

I never figured it out.

Once the birthday bookings are complete, I promptly ping an email to Luke. I think about the two brothers out for their mother's birthday. I find joy in the fact that I've turned an expensive yet mundane scarf into a remarkable and enchanting evening.

I begin counting down from sixty, and Luke enters the room before I reach five. "Woo-hoo! Dasia, you blow my mind and wallet."

"Just imagine the smile on her face." I give him an exaggerated grin.

"Thank you," he says, wearing a genuine smile. "She will absolutely adore this."

"My pleasure," I say, subtly studying his crow's-feet—evidence of a life lived with countless smiles. "And just to clarify, Jay isn't my boyfriend. Not that this is significant or anything. I just want to prevent possible misunderstandings."

He looks at me with intensity and nods. Then, without

a word, he spins on his heel and strides away, leaving me alone with my heart pounding as if it wants to jump out of my body.

I'm enjoying my "book time" on the commute home and looking forward to a quiet evening. Jay is cooking tonight.

Contentment fills me as I walk into our home and hear the clattering of a knife against the wooden cutting board. Jay hums. Outside, rain patters softly. All blissful sounds. A delicious smell lingers in the air, and all my senses start dancing.

I always think of music when Jay is in the kitchen. From a distance, I watch him. He's a master of edible art. A composer of masterpieces. He flows and rocks back and forth, lost in the moment, and the tapping rain joins the rhythm of his steps. He's preparing an emotional dinner.

"Hey, handsome," I say, entering the kitchen. "Whatever you're cooking has already sent me to heaven."

Jay looks up, still holding both handles of the stainless steel mezzaluna. His eyes are red and sad.

I frown with concern. "Are you okay?"

Jay walks over and kisses me on the cheek. "I'm making an open-your-soul dinner." He steps back to the counter and rocks the blades back and forth. Pushed to one side of the board are finely chopped herbs.

Sometimes during our meals, one of us will talk while the other just listens—no chiming in, questions, or comments. I've never encountered anyone who listens as intently as Jay.

I sit at the kitchen table, waiting for our open-your-soul-dinner to begin.

Jay finishes preparing our delectable meal and takes a seat directly across from me. "Here's to Ambrosia and to us," he says, raising his glass.

"To who?"

"Ambrosia—the food and drink of the gods."

I clink the rim of my glass against his. "To Ambrosia and to us."

The sadness in his eyes is reflected in his posture. His shoulders droop as if he carries the weight of the world upon them.

"Tell me as it is, Jay. I'm listening."

He explains that he recently completed a project for a famous client.

A few months ago, he'd been over the moon when he told me he really liked someone and that they might be a celebrity.

"I dared to let myself care for someone for the first time. Remember how I told you he was flirting with me nonstop? Anyway, I was hesitant to get romantically involved with him because he was a customer, but he phoned me today and asked if I wanted to go away for the weekend. We haven't even had our first date and he treats me like a . . ." He turns his face away, but not before I catch sight of the gathering tears. Moved by his vulnerability, I approach and embrace him in a comforting hug.

"Dasia, I don't know how you do it. Your hugs make the sadness just flow out of me and into the air."

I tighten my embrace. "He might have meant a romantic weekend, Jay."

"No. It gets worse. He also told me he's in a relationship." Jay wipes his eyes with the back of his hand.

"Bastard," I utter, taking a step back. Rarely do I curse, but this is warranted. I vow to stop watching the guy's Netflix series. "People are shallow, Jay. It's a blessing that you found out now rather than later."

He nods. "I know. I'm still processing the shock of his indecent proposal." He chuckles, and I join him.

"Shall we go to Columbia Road Flower Market on Sunday morning to soak East London into our souls? What do you say?"

Jay plays with the edge of the napkin on his lap. "I moved away from home to live life to the fullest," he said, glancing up at me. "I just yearn to find love. I long for someone who'll embrace me unconditionally. Someone who'll love me for exactly who I am."

His expression becomes gloomy and sorrowful, and he fixes his gaze on his plate. "Do I want too much, Dasia? The gay dating scene in London is harsh. People aren't genuine, and I'm losing hope that I'll find love."

He suddenly looks up. "Maybe I should have settled down with that girl my mother found for me."

I try to hold back, but I can't help letting out a laugh. "You realize that every part of that sentence is hilarious."

He laughs. I sigh. I wish I could take his pain away.

"Jay, you'll meet the right person one day. I know it. Just be ready to love and be loved, and don't ever forget that you are the love."

I look at the quote on our fridge magnet.

"Let your teacher be love itself." ~ Rumi

And you remember that too, I tell myself sternly. Jay catches me glancing at the magnet, and asks, "Do you think he said that exactly?" he asks.

I pause and respond, "I'm not sure; that was during the 13th century. Even if this is a variation of his quote, I still like it."

"If love were my teacher, what would I learn right now?" Jay asks.

"Hmm, let's see. First, you'd learn to be grateful that you found the love of your fabulous roommate, and that you're going to get a bucketful of beautiful flowers from a Sunday-only flower market."

Jay looks at me again. "I shouldn't have said that I haven't found love. It surrounds me in various forms. My siblings and my friends all shower me with their love. Even nature gives me love. And I'm incredibly grateful to have you as a friend, Dasia."

"It's perfectly all right, Jay. We all yearn for that special someone."

Silence falls with a stillness that's almost a sound itself.

Then Jay's breathing becomes heavy. "My best friend disowned me when I told him who I was. I was only seventeen. After he rejected me, I didn't dare get close to anyone for a few years. I felt this small." He creates a minuscule space between two fingers.

"Oh, Jay, I'm so sorry. What a lowlife. What's his name?"

"Jarrett."

"Please, don't let anyone ever make you feel small. You're an amazing person, and a great—a phenomenal friend to have. Jarrett is missing out."

Like my mother. She's the one missing out.

The sting of anger ripples through my body. I'm not sure who I'm most angry with, his best friend or my mother. I swallow my fury and focus on Jay again.

"Flowers, then? Let's get a 7:00 a.m. start on Sunday," I say with a wink.

Jay throws a small piece of ice from his glass at me.

"It's settled. We get up early to be at the flower market by eight.

Jay shrieks. "East London at 8:00 a.m.? Do I need to remind you that we live in very North London?"

"Exactly," I say. "So we must start our journey by seven. The market closes in the early afternoon. We're going to soak up those flowers, whatever the weather brings—snow, rain, or hail."

Jay looks at me, the left corner of his lip moving upwards. "Thank you."

"Anything to make my friend happy."

I seem to be getting into the habit of making people happy, and this fills me with a greater sense of happiness. But I really don't like that Jarrett guy.

On Sunday morning, my alarm goes off, and I'm confused as I look out my window. It's not even dawn. Then I remember that today is flower market day. I jump out of my bed and almost trip over my slippers. Columbia Road Flower Market is one of London's best street markets, and it's been on my things-to-do-in-London list forever.

After indulging in a steaming shower, I make my way back to my room to discover a petite bird perched on the windowsill. "Hello, little bird, how are you this morning?" I say warmly.

As the bird takes flight, an invigorating sensation fills me, as if I, too, possess the ability to soar through the skies. Playfully, I reach behind my back to see if, by chance, a pair of wings has sprouted.

"You just checked to see if you have wings, Dasia!" I say, a laugh escaping me. I need to go easy on the wine for a while.

After getting dressed, I knock on Jay's door. "Jay, wake up! It's flower market day." I hear some incoherent

murmuring. "I'll brew us some coffee. We need to be out
in thirty minutes."

"You're running a tight schedule here!" Jay shouts.

Just before we leave, my phone dings.

Who would be texting me at 7:00 a.m. on a Sunday?

I notice the tiniest tremble in my hand when I see
Luke's name.

> Thanks for helping with the birthday
> planning. She loved everything and said
> it was the best birthday ever. My brother
> was also impressed.

> My pleasure. Glad she liked it.

He's a thoughtful son, yet he's undermining Sarah. Is it
possible for someone to be both good and bad
simultaneously?

Chapter Twenty

Monday morning, my feet ache from yesterday's excursion to the flower market, yet I harbor no complaints. The experience was worth every step.

Before we even reached the market, its aromatic scents tantalized our senses. As we drew closer, our eyes were met with flowers, bulbs, herbs, plants, and an explosion of vivid colors. The camaraderie among the stall owners was like a mesmerizing performance, and the market hummed with people from diverse backgrounds. The whole atmosphere was infused with vibrant and lively energy.

We enjoyed delicious street food for lunch and then wandered the winding streets of East London, discovering small alleys, cute cafés, and stunning street art. I treated myself to two cute bonsai trees with charming pink flowers.

Feeling as if there's a marvelous week ahead of me, I twist the hot-water tap in the shower. All that greets me is a hiss. I turn the knob furiously, right, then left, then right again, but to no avail. This happened once before, and the landlord had to call a plumber. I take the fastest shower possible in icy water.

Shivering uncontrollably, I hastily wrap myself in a towel and sprint back to my room. I stand close to the radiator underneath my window to warm up. The birds in the trees look cold, too. At least they're wrapped up in their feathers.

"Ouch!" I cry out, as searing agony slices through my thigh like a fiery blade. I accidentally brushed my bare skin against the hot radiator.

"All right, let's select the perfect outfit to kick-start the week!" I say out loud, determined to mask the less-than-ideal start to my morning.

I spot my short black dress and decide to pair it with a three-quarter sleeve jacket in a stunning burnt yellow that reminds me of dusk and dawn colors. My mood immediately begins to improve.

I slip into my dress and yelp as I zip it up—my hair is caught in the unforgiving clasp of the back zipper.

"Okay, Monday morning, I dare you!" I declare, after releasing my hair.

Moments before leaving the house, I delicately nestle the bonsai trees within a spacious bag. Venturing into the rush of morning commuters, I manage to secure an unoccupied seat on the train. But just as I sit down, I see a pregnant lady standing beside me. I can't let her stand, so I offer her my seat and end up standing on the packed train, feeling the weight of the small trees in my bag.

As I exit the station, hailstones suddenly descend, pelting down around me.

What next?

I break into a run toward the office building. Huge raindrops hit my nose as I make my way through the main doors.

I see Luke by the elevator. I almost halt, but he sees me.

"Luke."

"Dasia."

Do I catch a slight spark in his eyes?

He looks down at my bag. "Are they real?"

"Miniature but real."

What spark? I think. *He's just his usual self.*

The elevator takes an eternity to arrive.

"How was your weekend?" he asks, as we finally step inside.

"I bought these bonsai trees. They're known to radiate balance, light, and harmony."

"Oh, okay." He reaches toward me. "You've got a small piece of hail stuck in your hair."

"It's all right," I say, pulling back. "It feels refreshing. Have a great Monday, Luke." I exit the elevator as swiftly as an arrow from its bow. I need to get to my desk and give Monday morning yet another chance.

On the way, I stop in front of Sarah's office. The door

143

is open, and she's sitting at her desk holding her head in both hands.

"Sarah . . . Are you okay?"

She looks up. "Something terrible happened, Dasia. The automation system crashed and made a mess of all the outpatient appointments and bookings." She closes her eyes and touches her forehead with her fingers.

"Give me a minute. I'll be right back." I quickly drop my purse, coat, and bonsai trees on my desk and return to her office.

She looks defeated. "I just reported it to the tech team. They're sending someone in. But, unfortunately, the crash wiped out the appointment-booking system."

Luke walks in with Emilia, and everyone talks at once. How, why, who, when, where.

"Sarah, can I use your computer?" I ask. She moves from her seat, and I sit and access the automation-project software. I contemplate the risk I'm taking but quickly brush my worries aside, reminding myself that I'm helping Sarah and the people at the hospital. I perform a system scan.

"It looks like the crash was caused by a virus," I say. "I'll call the software team. I can help them monitor network traffic." I'm dialing the number when I realize that I must sound overconfident.

The room has gone silent, and the three of them are looking at me with wide eyes. *Think fast and focus*, I tell myself. Everyone is still staring. While I wait for someone from the software team to answer my call, I say, "I like software, and I learned a great deal while supporting the automation project. I meant that it might be a virus, but I'm unsure." I'm certain it's a virus.

"I'll explain it to the tech team," I murmur, as they continue looking at me questioningly. Sarah's look is tinged with curiosity, but Emilia's is a little hostile. I don't want to look at Luke. Finally, someone picks up. I explain the situation to him, trying to ignore all the eyes on me.

The software team gets right to work, and Sarah and Luke rush to the South London Outpatient Hospital to help the team there. They're worried that patients will be in distress and staff panicking.

Luckily, the software team removes the virus by noon, and the automation system starts working again. But my heart continues to flip, jump, hop, and spring as if it's on a trampoline. I did more than call the software team. I helped them to detect the virus and manually delete infected files.

Once everything settles, I leave the office building to walk by the river. I can't eat anything, as my tummy has joined my heart in the acrobatics.

Did I risk too much too soon?

Walking back to my desk, I hear Sarah's voice. She's back from the hospital. I peek in. "Hi, Sarah."

"Come in, Dasia," she says warmly. "Thank you so much for all you did today! I knew it was the right decision to persuade you to stay, and I'm sure you'll continue surprising me with your abilities. That was a great intervention."

As she rises and gives me a hug, I inhale her scent, imprinting it deep into my lungs, knowing all too well that this may be our final embrace. It's only a matter of time before she learns about my past.

Chapter Twenty-One

L ife at work has been less eventful since the virus incident a few weeks ago, and spring is dramatically blooming in London. I notice how beautiful the parks and gardens look during this time of the year, and it's still only the end of March.

It's time to meet the teams at the hospital to discuss the changes the program will bring. Clinicians, nurses, doctors, administrative staff, and managers—we'll work with them to help create the best patient experience. Again, the image of a rowing team comes to my mind. Only with teamwork will we get the best possible outcome.

When we arrive at the hospital, we find our event space and prepare for the workshop. I've requested that the tables be arranged in an L shape so that people can see one another when seated. The attendees start arriving and everyone is friendly, having chitchats, except for one person. He has a standoffish posture and is frowning. He leans on the windowsill, his thumbs in his pockets, not interacting with anyone.

Everybody settles in their seats. With a genuine smile, Sarah begins the workshop.

The standoffish man sits and immediately raises his hand. "I'm happy with my booking system of thirty years. It works for my department. Why are we changing it? I should be caring for my patients instead of wasting my time here listening to management."

I watch Sarah with worry. This meeting has gotten off to a bad start.

But Sarah responds calmly. "Mr. Davies—can I call you Mike?"

He nods. I'm so glad that we insisted on name tags.

"I'm really sorry to hear this," Sarah says. "I'll stay after the meeting to talk with you or arrange a time to visit your department." Mike attempts to interrupt, but Sarah is firm. "We'll run the workshop as planned and address your concerns afterward. Thank you for sharing them. We also have regular events where people can share concerns." Sarah looks at me. "Dasia will forward the dates and times of those events."

Sarah then continues the workshop. I admire her leadership style. She wasn't defensive; she kept calm and provided information. How respectful she was.

I look at Mike to see that he's no longer frowning. He seems intrigued, and I see respect in his eyes as he looks at Sarah.

Mr. I'm Not Your Friend doesn't say another word, and he stays until the end of the workshop.

Afterward, Sarah approaches him. "Mike, can we arrange a time for me to visit you?"

He appears surprised. "Yes, I have my administrative afternoons on Wednesdays. I'll be in my office."

"Great, I'll be at your office on Wednesday at 1:00 p.m."

"Okay." He takes a step away then stops. "Thank you," he says, before leaving the room.

On our way back to the office, I ask Sarah, "How did you stay so calm? You didn't even challenge him when he was hostile."

She takes a deep breath. "I saw his pain, Dasia. I listened to what he was saying beyond his words. I worked as a nurse manager for years, and I know that look. He cares for his team and patients and is likely afraid of change. He has nothing against me personally. His approach was less than desirable, but recognizing and acknowledging pain is part of leading change. Listening beyond words is the essence of being a good leader and a compassionate human being."

What Sarah says makes me think about what my mother once told me: "Stop being so selfish. You're not the be-all and end-all of your father's life." I wonder what was beyond those words. Maybe, deep down, she was sad that she wasn't at the center of my dad's universe.

～

Luke stalks up to us as we enter the corridor. "Can we have a quick catch-up, Dasia?" he says sternly. "It's urgent."

"Let me drop off this project equipment first," I reply, trying not to sound irritated. We use portable projectors at meetings, so we make use of any available meeting room at the hospitals. I drop the bag at the project office then head to Luke's. "We had a long day at the hospital, meeting with the team," I explain. "I just got back."

"I know, but as I said, this is urgent." His tone makes me uncomfortable. "The project report for the executive team didn't have the right cover page."

There was an executive meeting this morning, and I'd prepared the project updates for it. Instead of using the standard cover page, I created a vibrant one that I'd thought illustrated the project journey. I'd shared it with the project leads and had meant to show Luke. Ultimately, I emailed it to all the executives without checking with Luke because I was in a hurry.

"It's only the cover page. You approved the rest of it."

"You must always use the standard cover, Dasia."

I stand in front of his desk feeling as if I'm in the principal's office about to receive detention. I look down. My black patent-leather shoes are pinching my toes. "The project leads agreed with the cover choice. It was a consensus decision."

His voice rises a few decibels. "I didn't see nor approve this cover page." He shakes it. I look at him for a second then silently leave his office.

I stare at an email from Luke the next day. It was sent to the whole team—a reminder that we need to use the standard cover page for the project updates.

"How to kill team creativity 101," I grumble, not realizing Charlene is standing beside my desk. She's walking in circles around the office, to get in her daily steps.

"What's happened?" She sits.

"Nothing. The cover page for the project report. Luke was unhappy that we changed it."

"That's because Mr. Goodwin insists on seeing the approved cover. He gets angry if he doesn't."

"I thought it was Luke who was angry about it."

"No, he's just trying to prevent upsetting Mr. Goodwin, so he won't be in a foul mood at the meetings. It's awful."

"I see," I say quietly. "But why wouldn't Luke say anything?"

"I guess he's uncomfortable that the CEO insists on a silly cover page."

Good news finally arrives toward the end of the week. When I walk into the office on Thursday, Sarah rushes out of her office waving some papers.

"Look, Dasia, we did it! These are the results of the first automation tests. They're very positive."

We walk together toward her office, and I see the bonsai tree with its tiny pink blooms on her desk in the middle of various family photos. My bonsai tree remains the only personal item on my desk.

"Let's share this with the team during our huddle today," she says excitedly.

I love our huddles, where we speak openly and honestly. Anyone can raise an issue without fear of being judged or challenged. And we actually huddle, standing close to each other.

I wish my family had done something similar when I was growing up. I wish my mother would have gathered us all in the kitchen so we could tell one another what was on our minds. I close my eyes and visualize what we would have said.

I would have voiced my wish for more quality time with her. My brother might have requested more opportunities to explore and roam to his heart's content. My father likely would have asked for additional family trips to create memories.

A weight bears down on my chest as I realize I don't know what my mother would have wished for. It suddenly dawns on me that I know very little about her.

Chapter Twenty-Two

My dearest Eli,

I was thinking about your dreams and hopes, about how you planned on traveling the world, going to the North and South Poles. Do you still have those dreams and hopes?

Lately, I can't stop thinking about Mom and why she isolated herself in her own sad little world. Have you ever asked her? I'm just curious about her story, you know? Like, why was she always so sad?

I often think of William, too, and I miss him. But knowing that he's better off not married to me gives me comfort. I sometimes peek into his cousin's social media pages, to see if he's posted anything that mentions William. I cried when I saw a picture of William smiling at a social gathering with his friends. He still has that charming smile.

I must go to bed now.

Good night, Eli.

The workday begins, and the pace is already hectic, even though it's not yet 9:00 a.m.

Sarah comes into the project-team office and sits next to me. "Dasia, can you help me, please?" She hands me her tablet. "I can't get the project page working again."

"I'll have a look. Give me a few minutes."

I love that she comes to me when she's stuck. But today, she seems distracted. She looks out the window then turns to me. "Shall we have lunch together? Let's walk to Borough Market. How about we leave at twelve thirty?"

"Of course."

At 12:25, we step into the elevator. Sarah's hand moves slowly to press the L button, and her gaze and her finger stay on the button for a few seconds.

"Imagine if we had buttons for life. You press, and things change as you desire." She removes her finger.

I wonder what she's getting at but decide to wait until lunch to see if she says more.

London's sunny and blue skies seem to signal the end of a long winter. Sarah is quiet on our walk. When we get to our favorite café, we find a table at the back. The menu is full of options for a light lunch, and we both order a pasta dish. We chitchat until our food arrives.

As I eagerly spear a bite of pasta with my fork, Sarah spits out, "My husband wants a divorce."

"Huh?" I manage to utter in response, before taking a moment to collect myself. "I'm so sorry to hear that. How are you holding up?"

Sarah pushes her linguini around on her plate. "I shouldn't be surprised. He was unhappy when I took the executive role." I see tears gathering on her eyelashes. "As I said to you before, women have to navigate a lot in life," she remarks, gazing downward.

"Not long after I began working as a nurse, I crossed paths with him and soon enough we were deeply in love," Sarah says with a smile. "That was almost 40 years ago. But things turned when he suggested that I quit my job. He was a successful attorney, came from a wealthy family, and didn't understand why I wanted to work. I thrive on making my own choices. My dad instilled this in me. So I knew I had to end things." Her breathing is slow, and her face wears a heavy expression as she looks at her plate.

"His insistence that I become a housewife ended up pushing me away from him." Sarah pauses. "Nothing wrong with being a housewife or full-time mother, of course. But it wasn't my choice. He didn't understand me at all. I didn't long for the big house and the comfortable life he offered. I was in love with him, not his background. What I truly desired was his respect." She continues looking at her plate.

"He realized that he was wrong. He apologized and we

got back together and never looked back." She pushes her linguini around again.

I don't say a thing. I don't eat. I'm there, just listening. Her gaze is fixed on the linguini. Finally, she puts the fork down.

"He recently retired, and he's not adjusting well. He hoped I'd retire too, and he was angry at first then really sad when I accepted my promotion. Now he's asked for a divorce."

She finally looks up and meets my attentive eyes.

"My parents had to put in long, hard hours of work, sometimes juggling two jobs, just to provide for our family and ensure our education," she explains. "My job is a source of pride and fulfillment, and I loved my time as a nurse."

I nod.

"Thanks for listening, Dasia. You're a great listener." She looks at my barely eaten dish. "I'm sorry for turning our lovely lunch into a downer."

"Thank you for sharing."

She inhales. "And thanks for not asking questions. In fact, thanks for not saying a word."

As we walk back to the office, I think about Christmas Day. At one point, when Sarah was out of the room, her husband inquired about our work and the automation project but abruptly changed the topic when Sarah appeared. Even though it had seemed a bit strange, I'd thought nothing more of it.

The automation project continues to develop well. It's been a while since I felt proud of something. I can't help but keep checking the reports, data, graphs, and customer feedback. I even take pictures of the charts to remind myself of our success. Having them on my phone allows me to bask in my accomplishments whenever I want. We even received feedback from patients who took part in the testing stage. Most said that the appointment-booking process had vastly improved.

I think about the times when I felt proud in the past. I was a valedictorian obsessed with pursuing a career in technology. My father and I celebrated for days after I received my acceptance letter from my dream college. My hard work had paid off, and I couldn't wait to attend the perfect college.

I saw my college education as an opportunity to prove to the world—and especially to my mother—that I could be more than just my brother's right-hand woman.

Then I fell in love, too. Every time I think about how I met William, a broad grin spreads across my face. I was at the library, on the brink of dozing off at a study desk, when I heard his soft voice and felt a gentle tap on my shoulder.

"Shall we step outside for a few minutes? Even the brightest smile and prettiest eyes need fresh air. Especially at 5:00 a.m."

Exhausted by hours of study and research, I thought I was dreaming. As we stepped outside, the sun was beginning to rise over Cambridge. The air was crisp, but I felt warm.

I was surprised by my mother's disapproval of William. "You never get it right, do you? We're paying your college fees so you can study, not date." Well, I studied and dated. I even received an innovation award for one of my research projects.

Reminiscing about my college days always brings me joy. I'd had the freedom to learn and excel at what I was passionate about, and everything had felt right. I'm surprised to feel a similar sense of being in the right place when I'm around Sarah at work. I never thought I'd experience a sense of belonging anywhere other than next to my father or on the MIT campus.

After the accident, I created barriers between the outside world and me. But now, I feel as if I'm slowly daring to peek around them. I notice daisies and daffodils, and I've started to savor little moments of happiness.

But I must never forget what I did.

Inspired by the thought of flowers, I snatch my phone from my desk and promptly change the wallpaper to a snapshot of the beautiful daisies I captured at the flower market one Sunday morning.

The stall owner had told me that *daisy* means "eye of the day." "They open their flower eyes in the morning and close them with the sunset," he said. I gently brushed my fingers against the yellow disk at its center, carefully studying the minuscule tubes. "Those little yellow tubes are the real flower, but you must have a keen eye to see them."

"How marvelous it would be if we could always see beyond what meets the eye," I remarked.

With a wink and a grin, he replied in his Cockney accent, "You have it, love. You already can."

Chapter Twenty-Three

Today is the first Sunday of April, I'm at the charity cycling event, the streets are buzzing with excitement. On Friday, I asked Sarah if she wanted to join me. She is familiar with Roy as his café is located near our offices.

"My husband and I are still navigating things," she said, explaining that they were actively seeking ways to move forward and find a resolution. Spending weekends together was proving beneficial for them. "Unfortunately, I won't be able to attend, but please tell Roy that I'm proud of him."

The roads on which the event will take place are closed to vehicles, and the map on my leaflet shows me the route. The cyclists will pass some of London's most iconic landmarks, such as Hyde Park, Buckingham Palace, Tate Modern, St Paul's Cathedral, and Tower Bridge.

The event is well organized, with plenty of volunteers

on hand to help guide participants and provide support at rest stops. What a fantastic way to unite people, support a good cause, and showcase what London offers. I'm thrilled to see that London is a nurturing city.

Every time I went to the café last week, Roy reminded me about the event. Though he shared the news with others too, he seemed to have a different energy whenever he spoke to me about it.

I join the crowd and cheer on each cyclist. I feel a surge of adrenaline when I see Roy, pedaling amidst a sea of hundreds of cyclists. It strikes me that I've only ever seen him at Pages and Beans. I can't help but notice that he looks rather dashing in his cycling outfit. He's beaming.

I wave and cheer him on, screaming his name at the top of my lungs, but he's unable to see or hear me. My gaze scans the ocean of faces— men and women, young and old. All the voices are united in a chorus of shouts. It feels as if every person on those bicycles is someone I know intimately. It's a moment that will stay with me forever. What an extraordinary day.

As I walk to the Tube station, I hear a familiar voice.

"Hey, Dasia!"

I turn around. It's Roy, wearing his medal and glowing.

"That was amazing!" I exclaim.

"Thank you! Do you have time for a quick drink before I catch up with family and friends?"

"Yeah, but I'm buying."

"How about we take a look at St. Katharine Docks?" he suggests. "There are plenty of options to choose from there."

It takes a while to find a place where we can get a seat, but I don't mind walking around, as St. Katharine Docks, near Tower Bridge, is a picturesque marina. Finally, we settle at a busy bar and I order our drinks.

"A charity cycle for children in need. How awesome is that?" I say, with amazement.

Roy looks at me as if he's just seen my face for the first time.

I return his stare with a smile. "What?"

"I adore the way you say 'awesome.' It's so quintessentially American."

I blush happily.

Then he touches his medal. His gaze is slightly distant. "I was one of those children in need."

"Oh, I see. Sorry . . . Uh, I mean, I don't mean sorry."

"Don't worry. Yeah, I was one, but a lucky one. There was a family who loved me and gave me a home, but many of my friends didn't have that."

"I'm so glad you found a family who loved you."

"I was still a mess for a few years. But they never stopped giving me another last chance—many chances." He smiles. "Boy, I was a troublemaker. My real mother died when I was a year old. My father worked away from home, kinda forgetting that he had a kid. I grew up with a stepmother and in different foster families until I was ten."

His eyes narrow. "I've seen firsthand what can happen when any Tom, Dick, or Harry can become a dad. So I'm all for putting potential fathers through some serious qualifying tests."

Our drinks arrive, and he takes a sip of his before he continues.

"Christmastime was the hardest. I kept running away from my foster families—I didn't want to stick around long enough for them to have a chance to give up on me. My wanderlust finally stopped with my last foster family. They chased me and never gave up on me." The lines at the sides of his eyes grow deeper. Then a big smile appears on his face.

"My foster mum is *awesome*." He chuckles. "I was ten years old when I met her. I remember my first day at her and her husband's place. They had a son, and I hated that kid. He had everything that I didn't. He was fifteen then."

I lean forward and gaze into his eyes, lost in the intensity of his childhood.

"I was sitting on the edge of a chair with my little black bin bag and a yellow fire truck in my hand. She came close, knelt, and said, 'Would you like to see your room?' In that moment, I recognized a truly caring pair of eyes."

He takes a deep breath. "She took my black bin bag from me and that was the last time I ever saw it. She held my hand as we went upstairs to my room, which is still my room today. Pajamas, a toy car, and a couple of T-shirts were waiting for me on the bed." He sighs. "I didn't know my life was about to change beyond my wildest dreams. Beyond the foster-kid kind of dreams."

"Dreams," I say, gently resting my hand on his arm. He glances at my hand then looks into my eyes.

"Yeah, today was about 'giving better bags' to foster children, so they don't have to move from one family to another with their belongings in a black bin bag."

To my surprise, I rise from my chair and embrace him. He hesitates at first, but then his strong arms wrap around me. He rests his chin on my head. I sink into his arms while getting a whiff of his scent. For a moment, everyone in the background fades.

He loosens his embrace suddenly, catching me off guard. Then he casts his eyes downward. In an instant, everyone reemerges in the background and reality settles back in.

Chapter Twenty-Four

My fast-paced workdays are also dictating life in my and Jay's apartment. We rarely spend time together anymore, as I leave early in the morning and return late in the evening.

It's a Sunday morning. In bed, I stretch and then curl up under my duvet.

I hear a whisper outside my door. "Are you awake, Dasia?"

"Yes, I am," I sing.

"Your morning coffee will be outside your door, Your Highness."

I chuckle. "Thank you for your kind thoughtfulness."

The presence of a true friend can be a game-changer in every aspect of life. It's been years since someone prepared a morning coffee for me. In college, I carried a little French press everywhere and made my own coffee. William, a tea man, attempted to make me coffee a few times, but you've got to love coffee to know how to create the wonderful experience of a good cup.

A thought creeps into my mind, making me feel uneasy. If I revealed my past to Jay, would he still make me morning coffees?

"Coffee by your door, and I'm taking you out for Sunday roast today. I miss you, Sparkles!"

When I lived with William in Oxford, we had a Sunday roast every weekend at my in-laws' house. I don't think we went a Sunday without it. During his recovery, William refused to socialize with anyone except his family. Every Sunday, I longed to catch a glimpse of the spark that had once lit up his eyes, but it never returned.

"Yay, Jay!" I call out. "Thank you!" It'll be great to catch up and have a traditional Sunday roast with Jay at a local pub. Jay's company has brought so much happiness into my life. "You're the best person in the world, and the most handsome, charming, and witty roommate in all of London." My voice resonates with happiness and hope.

Jay responds from the living room. "I always knew I was a catch, but I didn't realize I was THE catch of London. Thanks for letting me know."

I opt to adorn my ears with elegant emerald drop earrings for our outing. They hold sentimental value, as they were passed down to me from my grandmother. I feel a wave of confidence whenever I wear them. They make me feel prepared for anything. My grandmother was two years old when she and her parents left their home in Lebanon. They lived in Germany for a few years then

168

immigrated to the US during the Second World War. The stones are simply mesmerizing, and they reflect light most stunningly. It's almost as if they hold within them the courage and strength my grandmother and her family possessed. My father once told me that the earrings intensify my eyes and smile.

I decide to wear no makeup other than just the slightest bit of lipstick.

Jay and I leave shortly before noon, just as the clear weather turns into a windy spring shower. Trying to keep hold of the umbrella is like trying to hold a helium balloon in a hurricane—it's just not going to happen. I thank the heavens above for my makeup-free face, as no waterproof product would survive this type of rain. I think of the charity cycling event. The sky was a brilliant blue. What a lovely day for a race, and what a joy it was to spend time with Roy. There was clearly a spark there, though I'm still not sure why he stopped embracing me so suddenly.

"We can't control the weather, but we can control how we deal with it," says Jay. "Run!"

We duck our heads and plow through the gusts of wind until the pub appears. It's on the corner, and leading to the door are three broad steps with small square black-and-white tiles.

We hear laughter as soon as we step inside. It's a charming place with a low ceiling and a dark-wood interior. It's busy at the front and by the bar, but the host seats us in the small dining area at the side, where scents waft from the kitchen. Half of the dining area is occupied.

"Good that we arrived early," Jay says.

He's wearing a burnt-orange sweater with a slight V-neck that shows off his forever-tanned skin.

"You look buff," I say.

"Buff, right? How Brit is that? Thank you, and you look radiant today."

There's nothing quite like the feeling of receiving a compliment that comes from a place of sincerity and love. Jay is slowly removing the barriers of bricks around me with tenderness, care, and love. We humans are hardwired for love; it's coded into our DNA. The more I embrace this truth, the more exciting life becomes.

"I love these sorts of places for weekend lunches," Jay says. "Love that down-to-earth pub feeling and the delicious food." We both look around the place, and Jay points to a wall with a closed-up window. "Did you know there once was a property tax based on the number of windows in your house? See that window closed with bricks? Considering the pub is over five hundred years old, that could be why. Because of a two-shilling house tax."

"Are you serious?" I chuckle.

"Yeah, you see these closed windows on old buildings more often up North."

Our server approaches. She has beautiful light-red hair, smooth skin, and a few freckles on her nose. She greets us with a big smile.

"Ready to order?" he asks me.

A warm wave moves from my heart into my throat. "Orde-uh," I say.

"What's that?" Jay asks.

"Just admiring your Brit accent."

Jay and the server look puzzled momentarily, and then Jay orders. "Yes, can I please have the beef roast as it comes, with everything?"

"Same for me," I say.

The server strides away with grace.

"Did you have Sunday roasts as a family?" I ask Jay.

"Nah. I'm fourth-generation British Indian, but Sunday roast wasn't a tradition. Although growing up, I used to join a close friend at their family Sunday roasts."

His eyes go melancholy, and I know he's remembering his best buddy Jarrett, the one who abandoned him. He turns away and stares at the bricked-up glass. A moment later, his attention shifts to me. "You're an extraordinary friend, Dasia."

I reach for his hand. "You are too, Jay."

"I know I am, Dasia. But I'm unsure if you know how extraordinary you are."

"And so modest you are," I say with a laugh.

We chat about our childhoods and compare notes. I confidently declare that the pizza in New Jersey is hands down the best in the universe. "No exaggeration, my friend. It's true."

I tell him about my incredible father, and about my brother, who's the best brother one could ask for. To my surprise, I find myself opening up about my mother as well, delving into the complexities of our tumultuous relationship.

Jay demonstrates his Brummie accent, which features a downward intonation at the end of each sentence. It's just wonderful. In response to my insistence on hearing more, he explains that he always speaks with a trace of this accent. After that, I can hear it. I'm now aware of it. There are many things I've missed in the past few years. I make a mental note to visit Birmingham someday.

"Did you know that chicken tikka masala was created in Glasgow in the 1970s?" Jay says. "And the best tikka masala in the world is in Birmingham, not India."

We talk and talk. I laugh so hard at one point that I can't stop, and we notice people staring at us. "I think it's time to behave," I manage to say, while still laughing.

Our food arrives—perfectly roasted beef with potatoes, carrots, and peas. There's also Yorkshire pudding, which isn't a dessert but a savory side dish, like a popover. The aromas are intoxicating.

Jay points out the porcelain gravy boat. "No roast is complete without a jug of proper gravy."

Some things in life are sacred. Simple things. I pour gravy slowly over my roast. Jay does the same, and we dive further into the delicious world of Sunday roast and friendship.

We're having a cozy Sunday evening at home. Jay comes and sits next to me on the couch.

"I've got a feeling you fancy someone."

"I what?"

"You've got a crush on someone."

"Uh-uh, what do you mean?"

"You do, don't you?"

"Um . . . okay." I know there's no escape from Jay. "He's . . . He's just so down-to-earth," I murmur.

"That's how you describe your spicy feelings about a guy? I think he's the last person on earth I'd describe as down-to-earth."

"What? Who are you talking about?"

"Who are *you* talking about?"

Both of us blurt out a name at the same time.

"Luke!" he says.

"Roy!" I say.

"What?" we both shriek.

Feeling uneasy, I say, "You know Luke boils my blood, Jay."

"Exactly, my friend. Boiling blood doesn't always mean what you assume it does." He leans forward. "And Dasia, which guy are we talking about right now? Luke, not Roy." He winks.

"You're the worst, Jay!"

Chapter Twenty Five

I step out of the elevator into the office on Monday feeling confident. I'm wearing my drop earrings. Yesterday, I placed them on the nightstand beside my bed and fell asleep staring at them. I dreamed of life, courage, strength, and hope.

As I settle into Monday morning, touching the pretty little blooms of my bonsai tree, I hear Luke's voice.

"The tree missed you over the weekend, I think." He stands in front of my desk. I didn't even hear him approach. It's early, and just the two of us are in the project office.

"Good morning," I respond. His crisp white shirt peeks out from beneath his expensive-looking navy suit.

"Sarah and I are wondering if you could clear your day and support me."

"Oh, sure. I just checked my calendar."

"You check your calendar before you brew your coffee? I got you all wrong, Dasia."

"You have no idea how wrong," I say. Realizing how bold that sounds, I quickly shift the conversation to the matter at hand. "How can I help today? What do you need?"

"I'm leading a difficult conversation with a few powerful stakeholders. Nadia and I planned to cofacilitate, but she's having issues with childcare and can't be at work today."

Nadia is one of the junior managers on Luke's team. He doesn't seem to mind that she gave him so little notice. I would have expected him to be irritated at the inconvenience, but his calm and understanding demeanor suggests otherwise.

I grab my tablet. "I can be in your office in ten minutes. Will that work?"

"Are you brewing coffee first?"

"Yes," I say, without offering him one.

After a few seconds of silence, he asks, "Can I have one, too, please?"

"Sure," I say, with a victorious grin.

On my way, I peek into Sarah's office. "Taking marvelous-coffee orders. Would you be interested?"

She brightens. "I'd love one, please."

The three of us discuss the agenda for today's meeting as we sip our coffees. Sarah shares her insights regarding some of the individuals who'll be there. Luke seems uncomfortable. He'll be the one reporting to these stakeholders.

Sarah's gaze lingers on Luke. "Thank you for being supportive of Nadia," she says, her tone appreciative. "I can imagine how challenging it must be for her to raise a child on her own while juggling a busy work schedule."

Luke nods, his expression determined. "Her child is her top priority, and she'll always have my support, no matter what."

I watch Luke closely, noting his loyalty. This guy is like a complex puzzle waiting to be solved.

For today's meeting, Luke and I will need to travel to a hospital in Central London, which isn't far. Still, we'll need to leave early enough to arrive with plenty of time. The prospect of spending time alone with Luke makes my palms sweat, and my stomach flutters with anticipation.

At the train station, I check the Tube map and determine that we'll need to disembark at Euston Square after transferring at King's Cross station and changing lines. We step onto the crowded train and I feel the heat rising in my cheeks. The carriage is packed with people, and I'm forced to stand shoulder to shoulder, hip to hip with Luke.

As the train lurches forward and then halts, I stumble, and my hand shoots out to steady me. I accidentally place my hand on Luke's, which is gripping the pole.

I feel the electricity passing between us, and my heart skips a beat. Our eyes meet, and we're momentarily lost in each other.

I shake off the feeling and try to play it cool. I focus on the advertisements plastered on the walls of the train—anything to distract myself from the tension.

Noticing an ad for a new deodorant brand, I can't help but chuckle. "Check out that one," I say, nudging Luke with my elbow. "Looks like someone knew we'd be packed in here like sardines."

He grins at me. The train jolts forward once more, and I feel relieved that we're moving again.

King's Cross Station holds a special place in my heart, as it's next to the fabulous St. Pancras International station. Sometimes, I detour and get off at King's Cross to people-watch. The accents, the conversations, the various languages—these things never fail to captivate me. And I love the idea of ordinary and extraordinary people passing through the station, returning home, or rushing to work, each with a unique tale to tell.

St. Pancras International stands tall as an iconic gateway to Europe. I've heard tales of people hopping over to Paris for a leisurely lunch. The mere thought of such a luxurious experience makes me giddy with excitement. I promise myself that one day I'll spend time at the station, have a drink, and maybe even someday take the train to Paris with someone.

As quickly as the excitement bubbles up, the guilt sets in. I remind myself of my past, the pain, the hurt. I berate myself for even entertaining the idea and swiftly give it up.

When the meeting ends, it's almost 4:00 p.m. Luke and I are exhausted from the energy spent but also exhilarated by the successful outcome. When we reach King's Cross, Luke says, "Let's get out of here and get a celebratory drink."

And so, we step out of the train and walk through the busy tunnels to St. Pancras.

"The drink's on me," he says.

We take the escalator up, and I gasp at the scene. Every time, whichever entrance I use, the main area of the station never fails to take my breath away. It's crowded with people saying their hellos and goodbyes. Someone plays the piano, and there are art installations, buzzing shops, and cafés. We take the glass elevator up a floor and pass a bronze sculpture of a tall couple embracing each other.

"We're going to have a glass of champagne at the longest champagne bar in Europe," Luke says.

What I wished for only a few hours ago is now happening. Every day brings a new surprise.

"Sure," I manage to say.

We make our way to the bar. In this moment, I'm reminded that life is full of mysterious and powerful forces working together to bring our dreams into reality in ways that are beyond our understanding.

We sit at a table at the bar and order two Bellinis— champagne with fresh peach juice.

"Thank you, Luke. This is an unexpected treat." I frown a little. "But it's only four, which means we're still on the clock."

"Celebrating success is part of the project. We've had a heck of a day, and now we celebrate it."

I tuck my chin and toss my hair a bit. What am I doing? I must stop this flirting, as I'm still not sure I can trust him.

"Are you okay?" he asks, his tone spicy.

"I'm wonderful, thank you."

"That's for sure."

"Huh?"

Luke smiles and turns toward the bronze statue of the lovers embracing. "That statue is called the *Meeting Place*."

"When I see this statue, I think of the romance of travel," I remark.

"What do you like about the romance of travel?"

His enquiring eyes make me uneasy. It's as if he can see right through me. Warmth spreads through my body. For a moment, I fear he can sense that my heart is beating faster. His gaze lingers before he breaks the stare, and I take a sip of my champagne, relieved. But this is a peculiar moment—savoring champagne with Luke.

"So, tell me. What do you like about the romance of travel?"

I fix my eyes on the statue. "I love the hugs, goodbye tears, adventure, excitement, rough roads, ups and downs, journeys—and the companionship."

"Someone likes traveling." He has a soft expression.

"I love traveling, but I never really got around to doing

much of it, aside from moving to the UK. So I guess life didn't turn out as I'd hoped."

The hint of disappointment in my voice surprises me. Luke isn't exactly the type of person I typically have heart-to-heart conversations with.

Luke looks lost in thought, inspecting his glass. "What did you think of our session today?" he asks.

"Hmm . . ." I'm surprised by the change of subject. I think for a few seconds.

"Let's see. I noticed that many people cared more about being right than listening to and understanding each other's issues. It reminded me of my mother. She was always 'right,' and I could never persuade her to reevaluate her opinion."

I feel my cheeks getting hotter. How embarrassing to tell Luke about my family, especially my mother.

"Sorry," I say. "That wasn't what you asked."

"It's okay. I'm interested in hearing about your family. Do you have siblings?"

"Yes, a brother. He lives with my mother. I miss him. He's the best brother in the world."

"And your father?"

"Died the same year that I moved to the UK."

"I'm sorry to hear that, Dasia. It must have been terrible. Why did you move to the UK?"

"Circumstances. To be close to my ex-husband's family." I take a big sip of my cocktail, blinking a few times.

"You were married. I didn't know."

"Yeah, he was my college sweetheart." I quickly shift the focus to Luke. "How about you?"

"Did I ever get close to marriage? No, never."

"Your family?" I ask.

"Unfortunately, I also lost my father just before I was about to start college, and I never did go."

As I look into his eyes, I recognize that his sad expression looks like my brother's. My brother wanted to conquer the world but was stuck at home with our mother, leading the family business. His dream of exploring the world was replaced with responsibilities and duties. Our mother had groomed him for the role from a young age.

"Did you consider attending college as a mature student?" I ask.

"Nah, I don't have time for that. That boat sailed when I was seventeen. My mother and brother needed me."

"But boats do return to the harbors and sail out again," I say with a smile.

I think of my Sunday roast with Jay and the gravy boat.

A silence falls between us.

"Anyway," I say. "We should head back to the office. I have a long commute home afterward."

But Luke takes a sip of his drink and continues. "My father died in a freak horseback-riding accident. He fell, there was a rock, and that was it. It was tragic, especially considering he was healthy and only in his early forties. My mother went into a severe depression. I became the household's sole breadwinner. Without a college degree, I was at a disadvantage, so working hard was the only option."

"And you started as a care worker at one of the hospitals, right?"

"How do you know that?" he asks, raising his eyebrows.

"Sarah told me."

"Do you two talk about me often?" he says, with a glint in his eye.

I shake my head with a smile. He's so full of himself. "I used to think a college degree was the answer to many things in life. But our choices and actions shape our destiny more than a college degree ever could." I tilt my head, deep in thought.

"I chose to support my brother and pay for his college," he says.

I can't help but exclaim *Wow* inside my head. The man never fails to astonish me. His surprises come from every direction.

He studies me for a moment. "Right. Let's do this. I'll take the equipment back to the office. Where's the projector bag?"

I point to the chair beside me, a little perplexed by his suggestion.

"Okay, I'll take the equipment and you go home from here. We're already halfway to North London."

I feel unsettled. How does he know I live in North London? And why is he being so nice to me?

"Uh-huh." I glance at the sizable clock above the

statute. It's already past four thirty. "Um . . . okay. That would be great. I appreciate this, Luke. Thank you."

I urge myself to remain silent and not inquire, but the words slip out of my mouth anyway. "How did you know I live in North London?"

"You told me months ago, when we traveled together on the train."

"Ah, yes, I remember now." He wasn't intentionally trying to learn about me; he hadn't looked into my employee records or anything like that. It was just that brief encounter months ago.

I'm unsure of why I feel a twinge of disappointment.

Chapter Twenty-Six

A t work, time passes in a whirlwind. I can't
believe it's almost the end of May; the weather
has grown warmer, and the flowers are
blooming. The sun peeks through the clouds, making the
city gently glow. It's as if I'm seeing spring for the first
time. But is it because of the newly blossomed flowers,
me, or something else entirely? Maybe my perspective has
shifted in some way.

It's Monday morning. I take a deep breath and walk
into the office.

"Oh-hey, I need your help," cries Charlene. I can
almost hear the war drum in her voice.

"Let me drop my things." I jog to my desk, and she
follows. "Okay, tell me what you need," I say hurriedly.

"I urgently need to print a confidential document, but
my printer isn't working. Can I connect to yours? Once I
press print, I'll run and get the document. But can you

safeguard the printer and the document without touching it?"

"Go, go, go."

I stand by the printer, waiting for her document. A few minutes later she turns up, but there's no sign of the printout.

"Where is it?" she asks.

"Nothing printed, Charlene."

"Oh, no," she says, her voice trembling. "I must have sent it to the wrong printer."

"What printer?"

She becomes tearful. "I have no idea. Oh, this is bad. The document is strictly confidential. I never should have sent it to a different printer. But the meeting has already started, and Mr. Goodwin is waiting."

"How many printers do we have here?"

"At least ten." she shakes her head, and desperation flickers in her eyes like the lights on an emergency vehicle.

"Okay, you run and check the printers, and I'll try to locate the printer on your computer."

We run back to Charlene's computer. She unlocks the screen then takes off to check the printers, sprinting in her heels. After a few minutes, I locate the printer to which Charlene sent the document. Just as I'm about to dash off and search for her, I catch a glimpse of the document's title on her screen. "Oh," I say out loud.

Confidential Brief – Resizing and Managing Executive-Team Layoffs

I wonder if Sarah knows about this brief.

I can hear Charlene on the other side of the corridor; I run after her. "Charlene, Charlene!" I call out. She glances back but continues to stride forward. "It's one of the printers in the HR department," I shout, out of breath.

She runs so fast it's as if her heels transformed into buzzing sports car engines.

I hang around the meeting room, and when Charlene opens the door, I see Mr. Goodwin, Luke, and another male executive. Sarah isn't in attendance.

The automation project is progressing as planned. Questions arise within me: Why is there a confidential brief with a spine-chilling title? And why is Sarah conspicuously absent from this crucial-looking meeting?

A few minutes later, back at my desk, I pick up a call from Sarah. "Morning, Dasia. I'm at the South London Outpatient Hospital. I made my way here first thing this morning." She sounds distressed. "I left a message the project IT leads, please get them here—fast. There are issues, and I'm worried they'll impact patient care. The staff here are stressed out."

"What issues, Sarah?"

"The integration between the new and old systems aren't working, and it's affecting our appointment-booking systems."

"What can I do?"

"Nothing immediately. I spoke with Luke too. He'll join me here soon."

I want to tell her about the confidential brief and Mr.

187

Goodwin's meeting, but I decide to hold off until things have cooled down.

Sarah, I convince myself, will be fine. She's a leader with compassion and determination. She steps in and takes charge when necessary. Her genuine concern for others is what fuels her drive and ensures their well-being.

She reminds me of my father. Growing up, I watched as he poured his heart and soul into his work as an engineer, then as a business leader. But what impressed me most about my father's leadership was his compassion and care for his team members. He knew his staff were the company's backbone, and he did everything he could to ensure they felt valued and appreciated.

"You care way too much about your employees," my mother would say.

"There's no such thing," my father would respond, not taking his eyes off his newspaper. "They're family."

Just as my father cared deeply for his work family, Sarah extends her care not only toward me but also to others around her.

I immediately call the project IT lead, who tells me that they are already on their way out to meet Sarah. Feeling the need for hydration, I head to the office kitchen, where I see Luke and Emilia. Emilia is talking and giggling, but I don't hear Luke saying much.

"How unprofessional," I mutter. They should be attending to the crisis rather than spending time together in the kitchen.

I suddenly have the urge to take the matter into my own hands.

"Hello, hello," I say, my voice loud and sharp.

Emilia stares at me. Luke is filling a glass with water, and I notice a slight shift in his demeanor. He steps away from the water cooler, seeing the empty glass in my hand.

"Hello," Luke says.

Emilia doesn't say anything.

I start filling my glass. "It's a lovely day out."

"It's pouring rain outside." I can hear the irritation in Emilia's voice.

"Well, it's about perspective," I say, holding my full glass of water.

"Perspective doesn't change the fact that it'll be a miserable commute home," she hisses.

"We can't control the weather, Emilia," I say. "But we can control how we react to it."

"Whatever," she says dismissively.

I smile. "Rain doesn't have to be a source of misery. In fact, when it falls against a backdrop of blue skies, it can be quite breathtaking. A rainbow may follow."

They both look stunned, but Emilia also looks a bit hostile.

"Well, I have to go now," I say, turning around. As I walk away, I feel their gazes fixed on me.

I reach my desk, and tension mounts in my body. I kept my cool during the exchange, but now, I struggle to shake off the impact of it. I take a few deep breaths, trying to calm myself down.

Deep breath in. I count to eight. *Slowly exhale.* I count to five.

As I try to regulate my breathing, I can't help but wonder why I let their conversation get to me in the first place. I should leave Ms. Long Eyelashes and Mr. Flirtmeister alone. Next time I will.

My breathing slows, but the tension in my chest remains. I decide to access the project software to see if I can identify anything.

"Can we have a few minutes?" Luke appears at my desk; the set of his sharp jawline evokes dominance.

"I was checking the project pages. Can it wait awhile?"

"It won't be long." He scans the project office; a few team members are at their desks. "Let's go to my office." He beckons the way, and we start walking.

Well, well, well. It looks like I pushed someone's buttons in the kitchen.

I follow him closely. The scents of his tonka and cedarwood cologne—sweet, spicy, and woody—are as complex as he is.

In his office, we sit across from each other at his desk. I can't help but feel as if a storm is brewing within me. Seemingly unfazed, he leans forward, and I can feel the heat radiating from his body. This guy has a way of making me nervous and jittery.

"Right, so. So. Dasia, I know you've fixed a few tech issues here and there, and I'm really hoping you can look at the integration issues. They're impacting our service quality, and we only have a few days until the key board meeting. The project was going well, but this issue might cause a serious hurdle." He pauses. "The board might even vote to cease it. I've just spoken with Sarah and was getting myself a glass of water before heading out to meet her."

He locks his eyes on me as if he's trying to decipher all my secrets. "I somehow feel you might be able to help."

"That's beyond my skill set," I say, in a monotone voice. "It requires software capabilities and expertise." Meanwhile, my thoughts and emotions are in an uproar. I glance downward.

"I've seen what you've fixed before. Can you at least look at it?"

My skin crawls. I feel seen by him. I have ideas about how to fix the problem, and I want to help. But I break my excitement.

"I'm sorry, Luke. I can't help."

"You can't? Or you won't?"

I feel the color draining out of my face.

Before I can respond, he leans back and crosses his legs confidently. "Sorry, we're all stressed out about the integration issues. I didn't mean to upset you. It's okay. I'll join Sarah at the hospital shortly to see if I can help her."

I rise, and he looks at his computer screen. I accidentally glimpse his fingers as he types his password.

I remind myself that I took this contract to help Sarah. Despite the significant risk involved, I decide to look into the issues without telling anyone.

I'm nervous. I must proceed with caution. I'll remain

invisible and do what needs to be done. This is something I do well in life: remain unseen.

But first and foremost, I must satisfy my caffeine craving with a cup of coffee from Roy. Only then can I begin my secret quest.

Chapter Twenty-Seven

The afternoon has taken an unexpected twist. I find myself entering the hospital across the street from our office building clutching two cups of coffee—a small cortado and a large latte, not from Pages and Beans but from the café at the hospital.

I ask for the surgery department and follow the signs. Finally, I see Luke in the waiting room. His head looks as if it's bearing the weight of enormous pain. His hands are clenched between his knees. I'm hit with an overwhelming sense of sorrow.

As I approach, he lifts his head, and his tired eyes widen as he catches sight of me.

"Hey," I say. "I brought you coffee."

"What are you doing here?"

I hand him the latte.

At the office earlier, just as I was about to leave to get

coffee, a call came in for Luke. "He's at a meeting. May I take a message?" I asked, as I grabbed my notepad.

"This message is of the utmost urgency," said the voice on the other end of the line. "His brother has been admitted to the hospital and is undergoing critical surgery."

"Oh my . . ." It felt as though my heart flew out of my body. I took down the information and then hurried to the meeting room. At the door, I motioned to him, and in a split second, Luke was by my side, his hand on my shoulder.

"What happened? What's wrong?"

I swallowed a few times. My vocal cords were tangled, refusing to work together and make a sound.

"Dasia, I'm here. You're okay. Just tell me what's wrong. I'm right here next to you."

I faced him, and he placed both his hands on my shoulders, tightening his grip.

"Uhm . . . It's not about me. Luke . . . Your brother is at the hospital, having emergency surgery, and they want you to be there immediately."

After I gave him the details, Luke rushed out at the speed of light. Then I informed Sarah and hurriedly made my way to the hospital as well.

I sit next to Luke. He takes a few sips from his cup before quickly standing. He paces in an agitated manner, and his steps become quicker, his frustration visible in his movements.

"Typical of him, Dasia. Apparently, he was in pain for a day and didn't think of getting it checked until his appendix burst and almost poisoned him. I'll give him some pain in his head when he wakes up."

Grimacing, he slumps back into the chair next to me. I hesitantly place my hand on his knee. "I'm sure everything will be fine."

He puts his hand on top of my hand, and it feels as if a stream of lava travels from our hands and moves throughout my body. Then he turns his head to me and fixes his gaze on my face.

"Thank you. You didn't have to come here. You don't need to stay." He tightens his grip on my hand.

"Not happening. Sarah knows I'm here." I feel his thumb making little circles on my hand, and I don't think he even notices. Suddenly, he stands again. His eyes are sunken with pain. "I can't call my mother until I know he's okay. She'll be crushed."

Time seems to crawl as a doctor enters the room. We look into her eyes, waiting in agony. When she smiles, I take a deep breath.

"The surgery was successful. He's in recovery."

"May I see him now, please?" Luke pleads.

"You should be able to see him in a few hours."

The doctor leaves, and Luke drops into a chair. "I should call my mother."

Before he dials the number, I say, "I'll go now, but I'll be back."

When he looks at me again, it's as if there's no one else in the world besides us. "Thank you, Dasia."

On my way back to the office, I wonder why his

brother was in the area. When I return, I call Sarah. She's still attending to the fallout from the integration problems at the South London Outpatient Hospital.

"Don't worry about the work issues right now," she says. "Please offer all the support you can to Luke."

"Don't worry, Sarah. I'm right here to help Luke."

I draft a hospital-stay packing checklist then call Luke to tell him what's on it.

- Toiletries
- Phone charger
- Snacks
- Water
- Book
- Change of clothes

"Let me know what else to include," I say.

"A checklist for all occasions. You're every man's dream, Dasia."

"You're welcome, Luke. Good to know you still have your wit. Anyone I should alert?"

"No, my mother is on her way."

"No one? How about Emilia?"

"Especially not Emilia," he says, his voice as sharp as glass shards.

"Okay, see you in a bit."

Gosh, that question about Emilia really got to him. I'd

been under the impression that there was something going on between them.

I make my way back to the hospital and find Luke's brother's room. I knock on the door, but before I can turn the doorknob, Luke pulls it open, jarring my arm, and I stumble forward. His grip is strong as he holds me up with one arm, and I feel a rush of heat course through me. We stand there for a moment, not moving.

"Thank you," I say, straightening. "How is your brother?"

"Come and see for yourself."

My gaze slides toward the hospital bed, and I inhale a sharp breath, my lungs almost bursting from the shock. I squint, but what I see remains.

I step backward—right into Luke. I can feel his chest against my back, and his arms wrap around me to steady me once again. My face flushes, and I can't help but notice how muscular his arms feel.

"Oh my gosh, I'm so sorry!" I pivot and rush toward the bed. "Roy? Why are you here?" Settling myself at the edge of his bed, I gently clasp his hand.

Roy smiles. "Hey, Dasia."

I look back. Luke still stands by the door. "Luke's brother is also admitted here," I say.

"Yeah, that's me." Roy closes his eyes for a beat. I pull all my hair onto my right shoulder then shoot an inquiring look at Luke. He's now standing with his arms crossed.

"What's going on? Wait . . . What?"

"Do the math, please, Dasia," Luke says.

My mind races, searching for answers. "Uh . . . At this moment, two times two doesn't equal four."

They both chuckle, but Roy cringes with pain. Luke runs to him.

"Are you okay, mate?"

"Yes, big brother," says Roy, rolling his eyes and wearing the tiniest smile.

"How is that . . . Is he your brother?" I ask Luke, bewildered.

Luke looks at me. "Yes, Dasia. Meet my pain-in-my-backside brother. I believe you already know him."

"But this is Roy, from Pages and Beans Café." I'm still not following.

"Helloooo, Dasia," Roy says. "I'm still here."

"I'm so sorry, Roy, of course. How are you?" I gently touch his arm. His bed is surrounded by beeping machines, cables, and drips.

"You'll still like me even though he's my brother, right?" Roy winks at me. Then he adds, "Obviously, I'm the handsome one."

"Obviously," I say, smiling and stealing a glance at Luke.

"I thought Roy had a foster brother!"

Luke and I sit at the hospital café as Roy rests. Luke touches my hand, which rests on our small table. Only for a few seconds, but it feels as if time stops.

"I'm the foster brother. So, he told you about me."

"Yes, at the cycling charity event. But, neither of you mentioned this before. Why?"

"Do you two speak often?" His question catches me off guard.

"Sometimes," I say.

He stares at me. "This is on Roy. He didn't want anyone to know we were brothers." He looks away. "I stopped questioning his requests years ago. Only Sarah knows. Accepting someone's choices out of respect for them is always the best course of action, even if you don't agree with them or fully get their reasoning. I just want him to be happy, so I'll do what it takes."

Wow. This must require a lot of humility on his part. I fix my gaze on him. He seems adept at paying attention to his inner world, just as he pays attention to his outward appearance.

He sighs. "Roy had a challenging childhood. It took years for him to trust anyone. He was a handful as a child." Then he chuckles. "The little rascal made our family life pretty eventful. And he still gives me plenty to deal with. My parents applied to adopt him only a few months after we met him."

"So, Roy is the brother you supported."

"Yes. That's him. But trying to support him is another story. I'll need a strong drink when I tell you about that."

I reach for his hand, and he turns his gaze to me. I see the young man who gave up his dreams to support his mother and foster brother. I see a proud brother waiting at the hospital for his little brother. I see eyes that burn through me, and my heart starts flipping.

He looks down to our hands. "Dasia, I was terrified of losing him," he says, his voice breaking. His eyes are red and starting to moisten.

I place my other hand on his. "He's okay now, Luke. He's doing well."

"You know, growing up, he used to disappear, usually just before Christmas. It scared us all, but it broke my mother's heart. The final time he disappeared, he was thirteen, and my mother ended up in the hospital because of the worry. When he returned, he promised her that he'd never leave and that he'd always be close to her. He visits her every single week in Bristol. I mean, without fail. He longs to travel, and I wish he could, but he doesn't want to break his promise to our mother. He's thirty-four now but still as stubborn as he was when he was ten."

"Also, running a café must be demanding. Planning travel might not be easy."

He releases my hand with a slight frown. "The café was his choice. He has a hard time accepting help. He craves the freedom to travel. I've never met anyone who aches so much to see all the oceans and distant lands." Sadness crosses his face. "I keep telling him that standing on your own two feet doesn't have to mean being on your own. You can rely on others without feeling like a burden." He shakes his head a little and continues.

"He was never a burden to me. The first time I set eyes on him, he was sitting at the very edge of a chair in our living room. He was little for his age, and he clutched a toy fire engine as though his life depended on it. The burdens of the world pressed down on him, it seemed. His bright brown eyes met mine at that moment, and something within me stirred. It was as if I'd discovered a long-lost brother."

Tears well up in both of our eyes.

"He has this gravitational pull that draws people in," Luke says.

"That explains it," I murmur, thinking of the first day I saw Roy's warm eyes. "He's certainly passionate about his café."

"Yes, he is. It's his way of delving deep into life, people, and the world. His way of traveling, perhaps."

I smile. "He brings joy to everyone who steps into his café."

"Is that so?" He gives me a quizzical look, as if trying to read my thoughts.

"Absolutely," I reply cheerfully, picturing Roy and locking eyes with Luke as I try to decipher why my pulse is quickening.

"Get outta here!" Jay shrieks, when I tell him that Luke's brother is Roy. His jaw remains dropped for a few seconds. "No way!" He raises his hands to his face. "Wow, wow, wow, please elaborate! They're brothers!"

He moves about our living room, unable to stay still.

"Jay, you're making me dizzy! I had an exhausting day." I hold my head with both hands.

Jay stops and sits next to me. "Oh, my dear pumpkin, if you only knew. I've nothing to do with your dizziness."

I fix my gaze on him. "Well then, Mr. Know-It-All, enlighten me. What is it?"

He places his hand on my shoulder. "It's the dashing-brother love triangle," he sings, and scoots away from me.

"Stop it!" I yell, scanning my surroundings for an object to hurl at him. Despite my efforts, I can't suppress the smile on my face.

He vanishes into his room.

A true friend brings a smile, no matter what challenges life presents. I'm realizing that the more I let go, the better my life becomes.

I stop by Jay's bedroom, say good night, and command him to behave.

"As you wish, Sparkles," he shouts from behind his closed door.

Walking into my bedroom, I think about Jay's comment. With a determined wave of my hand, I declare aloud, "No dashing brothers!"

More firmly, I utter, "No dashing anything. No dashing allowed in my life."

Chapter Twenty-Eight

I t's been three days since his operation and Roy is
doing much better. Luke will be back to work
tomorrow. There's a critical board meeting, and
he'll demonstrate a live update of the automation project. I
now know the two things that matter to Luke: his work and
his family.

At the end of the day, he calls to ask me to look for a
file on his desk. As I step into his office, my heart beats
quickly. I'm not sure why.

I look for the report he mentioned but keep glancing at
his computer. I still remember his password, and I have an
overwhelming urge to find the secret report about
executive layoffs.

I convince myself I'm doing it for Sarah.

With a deep breath, I sit down in front of his computer
and type in his password: Chapt3rone.

Strange password, but don't we all have a few of

those? It could be a reference to Torone. Maybe Luke likes Greek mythology. The screen comes alive.

I quickly find a folder titled ***Confidential Brief – Resizing and Managing Executive-Team Layoffs***. I insert my flash drive and press download.

Suddenly, I hear footsteps drawing nearer. The bitter taste of terror floods my mouth. I eyeball the door and try to push down the panic rising in my chest.

"Ah, it's you, Eileen," I exclaim with relief.

The woman who cleans the offices peeks in. "Hello. Can I empty the trash?"

"Of course."

Eileen walks around the desk and takes the trash can. After emptying it, she places it back behind the desk but, in the process, knocks over a silver penholder. All the pens fly out.

"Ah, I'm sorry. I'll pick them up."

"It's okay, Eileen, I'll pick them up. You have a good evening."

After she leaves, I bend down to pick up the pens and notice a tiny key near the corner of the desk, on the floor. As I hold the key, I think that a key is never without a matching lock. I couldn't resist the magnetic pull of the unknown and my gaze darts around. "Aha!" I say, noticing a small locked drawer underneath Luke's desk.

I put the key in the lock and turn it to the right. Nothing happens. I turn the key to the left, and the drawer opens.

There's a journal inside. I touch the cover then take it out. I flip the pages.

Well, well, well, Luke. You're a diary-keeping sort of guy. Who would have thought?

Fighting the almost-irresistible temptation to read it, I slowly put the journal back. I grin, and my chest swells with pride for doing the right thing. Suddenly, my eyes are drawn to the inside of the drawer, and they widen in shock. My hands fly to my face, and I cup my falling jaw.

What am I seeing?

I reach out and take the photos slowly. There are two photos of me in the office kitchen, alone, and another one of Luke and me chatting in the kitchen. I'm surprised to see that I look like a woman enjoying his company.

I can't believe what I've found. With shaking hands, I place the photos back inside and lock the drawer.

I jolt at the sound of a thunderous ping. A chill grips my spine. Slowly, I realize it was just a notification on the computer. The download is complete. Still, my nerves remain on edge while I take my flash drive.

As I leave Luke's office, I recall why I was there in the first place. Avoiding the hidden drawer, I quickly return to retrieve the requested file.

I cautiously push open the door to Roy's hospital room the next morning. Roy lies in bed while Luke occupies a chair beside him. Both are asleep. It's impossible to ignore their differing rugged good looks. I take in their peaceful faces.

There's an intense throbbing in my core all of a sudden, and I silently drop the file and leave the room. I can't shake off the intense emotions leaving me feeling disoriented.

I hurriedly return to the office, determined to continue tackling the integration issues head-on. I've been working long hours the last few days, carefully addressing the problems from the background. Meanwhile, my head is busy juggling all the recent revelations. It's as if there are two versions of Luke—one is a loving and attentive brother, and the other is a manipulative executive who attends secretive meetings, hides essential reports and keeps secretive photos of me in his drawer. *Goodness me, who's this person?*

This week, my checklist for remaining composed includes repeating this mantra:

- *I am a calm and chill cucumber!*

When I leave the office building in the evening, I replay the last four days in my mind. My emotions feel as if they're all in a blender and someone has pressed the "confused" button. A good night's sleep is a must.

~

On Friday morning, I look at my reflection in the mirror in my bedroom. My attempt to get some rest turned into a spectacular dance with insomnia demons, and my tired eyes reveal my restless night. I dress to hide it, putting on a simple yet elegant dark-blue dress with long sleeves and a belt. It hits about an inch above my knees. I then peer at the pretty scarf box on the table.

My mind goes back to the time when my father and I went shopping for a birthday dress for me. My mother refused to come with us, saying that it was nonsense to make this much fuss about my sixth birthday. But for me, this birthday was a huge deal. It was the first time I was allowed to invite my friends. And for my mother, it was an opportunity to impress other moms by showing off our "perfect" home and family.

I fell in love with the pink dress as soon as I saw it. It was beautiful—a wild-rose-pink maxi dress with a tiered skirt, lace ruffles, flutter sleeves, and a straight neckline. My father gripped my hand and said, "I think your dress found you."

After school the day after my birthday, I raced upstairs to put on my dress again and froze by my door when I saw pink scraps scattered on the floor. I screamed at the top of my lungs and sat in the middle of the pieces of my beautiful dress.

My parents immediately gave my brother an earful. I peeked at him through my tears. He looked at me and shook his head so slowly that only I could see it. I never believed it was him. He denied it, but our mother told him it was bad to lie. He then became quiet. Dad wanted to buy me another dress immediately, but I didn't want one. Since then, I've refused to own any pink clothing.

Until yesterday.

While I was walking home from work, I spotted a pink scarf in a corner boutique in the arcade I walk through every day—the very shop at which Luke wanted to buy a scarf. Ah, life has a knack for unexpected twists and turns.

I stood still in front of the shop window and imagined the gentle caress of the pink silk against my face. Then I watched in my mind's eye as the scarf floated and waltzed through the air, all around the arcade.

I take the pink scarf out of its box and let the silky fabric flow over my hands before I tie it around my neck.

My dad always said, "If there's one thing you can count on in life, it's change."

Here stands a woman constantly transforming, I think, as I look at my reflection in the mirror.

I feel the weight of my emerald earrings as I greet some unfamiliar executives. We've moved from our usual meeting place to a larger space, much higher up in the building. Outside the window, far below us, people mill around like ants. This is a crucial gathering for Sarah and the automation project.

Luke sits on the other side of the table. Our eyes meet for a split second. He's wearing a tie I've never seen before. It's dark burgundy, contrasting his pale-blue shirt and navy trousers. Most of the men around the table are wearing darker suits.

Sarah starts her presentation. She has a calm manner and a clear voice. I was in awe when she shared the presentation with me earlier. She's delivering it through a patient's eyes, focusing on how the automation project is making a difference in patients' lives. To prepare, she spoke with patients and their families and spent time with staff members. Her passion for making a difference is all over the presentation.

Looking at Sarah, I see a caring and compassionate woman. I also see a determined woman who took a significant risk and leaped out of her comfort zone into the unknown to prevent job losses. I then study Mr. Goodwin. He's unusually quiet. He almost appears to be troubled by the project's success.

Luke is set to present the live automation to the board members, to show the improvements made on the project. He mentioned to me that he'd prepped a response and plan of action for any integration issues that might arise during his live demonstration. Sarah is nervous that the board might take a vote of no confidence in the automation once they see the integration issues across the old and new booking systems.

Luke begins his presentation, bringing the automation app to life on the screen. It works flawlessly, and I can tell he's stunned by how well everything clicks together without any hindrances. He blinks a few extra times but otherwise hides that he's perplexed. He locks his eyes with me again before he resumes.

Although I initially refused when Luke asked me to look into the integration issues, I did fix them. In the evenings, I checked every code, each piece of data, every update. And when I figured out the glitch, I did a little dance in the middle of the office.

The meeting concludes with the board members congratulating Sarah and Luke on their success.

Sarah beams at Luke and me. "This was a team effort. Thank you, Luke, for your leadership, and thank you, Dasia, for your coordination and input. And those earrings are stunning."

Luke looks at me and nods. He mouths, "Thank you."

My stomach drops as I realize that he's aware I solved the problems. Yet, at the same time, I'm happy he noticed.

Ignoring my inner turmoil, I stride back to my desk. The silk scarf flows, whisking away all my worries. I just want to take a peaceful moment at my desk and look out the windows. I hope that the project office is empty.

"Oh no!" I exclaim, stepping in.

My bonsai tree isn't on my desk but on the floor, and its pot is shattered. I crouch. "Oh, honey!"

Some branches are broken, but the tree is still okay. I sprint to Sarah's office, praying that her tree is okay, too. She's with someone, but I can see that her tree looks healthy and happy on her desk. I turn around before she can see me looking as if I just saw a ghost and holding a bonsai tree by its roots.

I have the sensation that someone's watching me. Maybe it was the office cleaning crew who knocked the tree over, but they only work in the evenings. It must have just been a weird accident. I gently brush the branches with my fingers.

"I'll replant you, and you'll feel better than before. I promise."

On Monday morning, bright and early, I repot my bonsai tree. It's now in a stunning handmade ceramic pot that emphasizes its beauty. The pot has oval edges. Normally I like straighter lines, but sometimes we must let go to appreciate different viewpoints.

Love changes you.

My colleagues and I decided, after a long debate, that it was a freak accident. That something somehow moved it from the back of my desk and caused it to crash to the ground.

I smile and touch its branches. "Thank you for letting me take care of you," I say. "It's healing for me too."

My gaze then falls upon a crinkled piece of paper on my desk. A river of dread runs through me as I reach for it.

Chapter Twenty-Nine

I stare at the jagged letters cut from magazines and arranged into a terrifying sentence.

I look around the office and suddenly feel as if I'm in a movie where my reality is becoming a twisted nightmare scene.

A threat. A broken pot. Photos of me in a secret drawer.

I place my left hand on my trembling right hand, which is holding the note, and stay still for a few seconds. Do they know my secret? How? I wrestle with different theories. Perhaps an intrepid journalist tracked me down. Or maybe someone conducted a deep dive into my background. But why?

I shove the note into a drawer in my desk and head for the bathroom. The weight of my wrongdoing has burdened me every single day since the accident. I've never been able to forgive myself for what I did, and I certainly don't need any reminders.

As I look into the mirror and meet my own eyes, panic intensifies within me. A sniffle escapes, and my panicky state dissolves into overwhelming sadness.

My time here has come to an end. I took the risky leap and fell flat on my face.

With shuffling footsteps, I begin what might be my last walk toward Sarah's office.

Sarah and Luke are having a Monday morning chitchat. They're still energized from the successful board meeting on Friday. I suddenly change my mind about talking to Sarah, but she sees me before I can retreat.

"Dasia, how was your weekend? Come on in and join us."

"Good morning," I say.

I glance at Luke, and his eyes meet mine. It feels as if he's like a giant magnet and I'm a small pin forced into his magnetic field.

My stomach ties itself into a knot. I suck in my tummy as the knot gets larger, expanding into my chest and rib cage.

Luke frowns. "Are you okay, Dasia?"

"Yes, I'm . . ."

I flee. My pulse thunders in my ears.

Around noon, Sarah comes to my desk. "You looked troubled this morning, Dasia. Are you okay?"

"I'm okay," I manage, mustering a reassuring expression.

She stares at me, and I know she sees right through my act. "I'm having lunch with Wesley today," she says, after a pause. "He's in town meeting his old work colleagues. So, I might be out a little longer, but start the afternoon huddle without me."

"Of course. Enjoy your lunch. I'll also take my lunch now."

Sarah recently mentioned that things have been improving at home. It's excellent news. I remember how, at Christmas, Sarah's husband had looked at her with admiration and love.

After Sarah leaves, I check the time. I have more than thirty minutes. I wonder if Roy is at the café. I haven't seen him since he was in the hospital. I fly down and flap into Pages and Beans, but Roy isn't around. I settle in my usual corner in the PAGES section after ordering my lunch.

"I understand, sir," a male voice says.

I pause before taking the first bite of my sandwich. Is

that Luke? I slowly turn around and see Sarah's husband on the other side of the wood panel that separates the PAGES section from the other tables.

"Son," Wesley says. "You know how much I love my wife—please help me get her home! I don't want her working twelve hours a day in the middle of the city. I want us to enjoy our lives and travel."

Still holding my sandwich, I run out of the café. Once I turn the corner, I stop and lean on a wall. I can't believe what I heard. The conversation plays in my mind like a broken record.

I understand, sir.
  Please help me get her home!

I place my hands over my ears, but the record keeps playing.

I understand, sir.
  Please help me get her home!

My desperation intensifies.

"Hey!" someone says loudly.

I startle—so much so that my sandwich takes a dive from my hand and lands on the ground.

"Dasia, what's up?"

Roy is standing in front of me, and I can't help but walk into his arms and burst into tears.

"Okay, okay, let's get you to the café," he says, but I

shake my head. I remain in his hold, where I feel safe. He tightens his embrace, as if he's reading my thoughts.

Moments later, I brush the tears away from my face and reluctantly step back, feeling sorrowful as I part from him. "I need to get back to the office."

It dawns on me that I stumbled into the arms of a man who was recently released from the hospital.

"Oh, no! Did I hurt you?" I ask, looking at his waist.

He grins, gesturing to his right side. "The op was here, but no, don't worry about it." He scans me, and I wish the brick wall behind me would swallow me up, so I'd disappear.

"Sorry, this is embarrassing," I say, though I don't feel bad about the hug. My attention shifts to his muscular arms and chest. "I've had one of those mornings."

"Nah, don't worry, nothing to be embarrassed about. Glad that I saw you here. Are you sure you're okay to return to work? Anything I can help you with?"

"No, I'm good. Thanks, Roy."

He gently tilts up my chin with his finger, and I feel a surge of heat travel through my body.

"Anytime you need a friend, okay?"

I nod and grin. Then I notice my lunch on the ground.

"Don't you worry," he says. "I'll pick it up."

I make my way back to the office lost in contemplation and feeling a sense of urgency. I need to share what I've just overheard with Sarah.

As soon as I reach my desk, my phone rings, and I startle again. It's Sarah.

"Dasia," she says. "How are you? Are you feeling better?"

"Yes, thanks."

"Just to let you know, I'm going to work remotely this afternoon. I'll see you in the morning."

Well, that changes things. I decide to postpone speaking with Sarah until tomorrow. I'll share every detail with her then.

- *I'm not the person she believes me to be.*
- *I single-handedly solved the integration issues without telling anyone.*
- *I caused irreparable damage to those around me in my past.*
- *I'm a computer-science engineer.*

But I'm unsure of how to break the news about her husband's deception. To add insult to injury, Luke isn't who Sarah believes him to be.

I have the confidential brief on my flash drive that I still haven't done anything with. Last week we were focused on resolving the integration issues and preparing for the board meeting. I didn't want to put additional stress on Sarah. But tomorrow I'll tell her what I know. I must finally disclose everything.

I take my eyes off the screen and look at the river below, feeling as though its flow mirrors the turbulent emotions within me. I'm jolted from my thoughts by the sound of footsteps approaching. I turn around in my seat and there stands Luke, towering over my desk. He sets down a neatly wrapped sandwich.

I attempt to contain the wave of anger rushing through my body. But it's no use. I stare at him, my eyes burning with fury.

"Whoa, what's up, Dasia?"

"Nothing. What's this?" I point at the sandwich.

"Uh, that. I now work as a delivery boy. That's your lunch order."

"I didn't order anything." I'm so angry with him that I can barely look at him.

"Roy told me to deliver this sandwich to Dasia, and you're the only Dasia here. You're the only Dasia I know in this entire universe."

"Thank you." I look at the sandwich and think of the comfort of Roy's arms.

Luke gives me a sidelong glance. The silence between us is so thick that I can hear his breath. He then stuffs his hands into his pockets and walks away.

I jot down my options.

- Option one: Admit the truth to Sarah and exit. Once she's aware, my presence in her life will be unwelcome.
- Option two: Remain and assist Sarah. Don't inform her of any of the deceptions, so she can concentrate on the work—the automation project is nearly complete. Strengthen ties with Luke.

But how much risk is too much?

Whoever wrote the note with the cut-out letters didn't reveal anything to anyone—at least I don't think they did.

I imagine gripping Luke's ankles and suspending him from the rooftop of the building. I swiftly pull him back, and he clutches me, expressing gratitude for not dropping him. Then, I picture Sarah, and I imagine cutting Luke's expensive suit jacket into hundreds of little pieces while laughing.

I already feel much better.

It's still Monday, Jay is away visiting his parents for a few days. In our apartment, I sing "I Will Survive" at the top of my lungs.

I've decided that I must keep the enemy close. And to do so, I need to work on my flirting skills.

I have my how-to list.

- Chin down
- Play with your hair
- Tilt your head
- Bite your lip
- Touch his arm for only a few seconds
- Let your gaze dart around

I practice in front of my mirror.

I heard somewhere that people who flirt a lot tend to have more white blood cells. *Luke's immune system must be very healthy.*

This is harder than I anticipated. It makes me sad that I thought I saw a kind, caring man at the hospital with his brother. How wrong I was—once again! The photos, the threatening note, the betrayal of Sarah. Oh dear, he almost had me.

I can't help but think about Roy, and how different he is from his brother.

I arrive at work the next day wearing wide-leg dark-brown trousers and a beige bow-tie blouse. My silky dark hair shines like a moon-glade on a still sea. I'm wearing a deep-pink lipstick rather than my usual light, natural-looking one, to make my lips look luscious.

I hold a mug of coffee, enjoying the warmth on my fingers. Blinking, I knock once and enter Luke's office.

221

"Good morning!" I sing.

Luke stands by the window, one hand in his pocket, looking out. He turns around.

"I brewed a different type of coffee today," I say, as I pull my hair behind my ear and bite my bottom lip with the intention of conveying a subtitle: *My heart wallops when I'm around you.*

He seems confused. "You look different today," he says.

Playfully swaying my hips, I walk close to him. "Different how?" I stare into his eyes.

"Ehm . . . You're just . . . different."

"Would you like a taste?" I ask.

He looks me up and down, and then his eyes lock on my lips.

"I think you do. Here." I hand over the mug, and as he sets it on his desk, I get a whiff of his cologne. It makes me a tad dizzy.

"Dasia, what are you doing to me?" he asks, his voice raspy. Moving away from the window, he strides toward me with inquisitive eyes, positioning himself in front of me. Placing his hand on the desk, he leans closer. The desk presses into my back, and his masculine body is an inch away from mine; I'm tightly wedged between. Every fiber in my body reacts. He's stealing my good sense.

Abort and take control!

"Tell me," he whispers, demanding an answer I dare not give.

I close my eyes for a beat and inhale the moment. I feel

222

alive. The current between our bodies ignites sparks all over me.

I quiver. *Abort and take control! Fast! NOW!*

I push against the desk attempting to create space between his body and mine, yet there seems to be no room left to spare. I lightly poke my index finger against his shoulder, he takes a step back. While a subtle smile curves on my lips, swiftly, I step out of his presence and leave his office.

I had him just as I wanted him. Just like that. Right there. But a storm of confusion engulfs me. Why do I feel so out of balance, despite my bravery?

Chapter Thirty

I shrink with nerves when I think about Luke's secret drawer. About the photos he must have obtained through security-camera footage. I bet he's very friendly with the security team. I suppose I could file a complaint with the HR department, but that would mean admitting I snooped around his desk. And I must prioritize Sarah.

The week turns into a meeting frenzy as we approach the automation project's final stages, and Sarah is in and out of the office.

On Friday morning, I stride into the office and change into my heels at my desk. Here I am, moving ahead with my mission. I walk heel to toe and take my time. My imaginary straight line is helping me to feel fabulous and graceful. I hear Luke's voice as he exits the elevator.

Keep the enemy closer! I remind myself.

He's on the other side of the corridor, but I know he's

approaching the kitchen. When I walk in, I immediately notice that my small coffee maker is gone. My grinder is also nowhere to be found. Did I walk into the wrong kitchen?

I look around, and my breathing becomes rapid when I see my items on the floor in the corner. Someone has cut the cord on my coffee maker and smashed the carafe into shards, and the coffee grinder is dented beyond repair. I kneel among the broken pieces.

"Blimey." Luke crouches next to me. "What the hell happened here?"

"I don't know. I just arrived a minute ago."

Luke offers his hand and helps me stand up.

"Who would do such a dreadful thing, Luke?" I open the cupboard in which I keep my coffee beans and see that the package has been punctured and slashed. "This is terrible!"

"Get security to the office kitchen!" Luke's voice reverberates around the room.

I turn and see Charlene darting away in a hurry. Other colleagues gather, murmuring.

"What on earth happened here?" Emilia exclaims.

As Sarah comes into view, the ache in my chest eases a little. She's followed by two security personnel.

Luke and I proceed to file our report. Then Luke says he'll treat everyone to coffee from Pages and Beans. Two people take orders.

"Don't mention this incident to anyone outside these

offices, understood?" Luke says to the group. "Let our legal department deal with it."

I'm confused, who would do such a thing. I bear no grudges against anyone.

Minutes later, the three of us sit in Sarah's office trying to make sense of it.

"Unfortunately, there're no security cameras in the kitchen," Luke says. "But it had to have been the last person leaving the office, as they would have made a lot of noise."

I frown a little. No security cameras in the kitchen. Then how did Luke get those photos I saw in his drawer? They were taken in the kitchen.

"My package of coffee was stabbed," I blurt. "Maybe someone wants to kill me."

"I don't think so," Luke says. "I think it's just some petty person who wanted to upset you."

"So now you're a seasoned detective? Have you solved similar cases in the past." I know I sound as irritated as I feel.

Sarah interjects. "The security team is investigating, and I'm sure they'll find out who did this awful thing. However, I must say I'm with Luke on this—whoever did it wanted to upset you and they knew how. Everyone on the floor knows that you have a coffee ritual in the morning. But also, everyone loves your coffees too, so the person might be upset with all of us.

"I suppose," I mutter, and get to my feet. "Thank you, Sarah, and I appreciate the coffee, Luke."

"Would you like to take the day off?" Sarah asks.

If you only knew, Sarah, I think. *Luke keeps pictures of me in his drawer, I'm being threatened, and your husband is trying to sabotage you with someone you trust.*

"I appreciate your concern, but I'm okay." I try not to glance at Luke as I leave Sarah's office.

My brother was obsessed with *The Art of War*, by Sun Tzu, and we used to memorize parts and enact battles in our backyard. I remember a line from the book, and it helps me to gather strength:

> "Let your plans be dark and impenetrable as night, when you move, and fall like a thunderbolt."

My plan is to keep my chin up as I build the strength to fall like a thunderbolt. I owe this to Sarah and other people here, and even to myself.

I stand tall to face the day; I must speak with Sarah.

I attempt to muffle the sound of my sobs in the office restroom. A couple of minutes prior, I attempted to strike my Wonder Woman pose, yet to my dismay, it had absolutely no impact.

There's a knock on the stall door.

"Dasia, is that you?" Sarah calls. "I won't pretend I didn't hear you, Dasia."

Earlier, I was holding a project-update meeting. I

sensed trouble when I saw a senior manager walk into the project-team office with two others.

I don't know him very well. He always sits next to Mr. Goodwin, nodding like those toy dogs on car dashboards. I think of him as Mr. Bitter because he always has something to complain about.

He walked in and stood behind us. I sensed his vulturelike gaze and turned around. "Please join us if you want to be updated on the project's progress," I said, beckoning him forward. "We've just started."

He didn't move. "Listen up, people," he shouted, in his nasally voice. "I'm sick and tired of this project. It's a disaster. Integration problems persist, and people are upset. With the GMs here, we demand answers. This is unacceptable, and I'm planning to contact the board to stop a full implementation."

We stood stunned as he stormed out of the office, taking the two general managers with him.

I looked around. Everyone appeared gobsmacked. Our positive huddle energy had vanished.

Sarah appeared—she probably heard the shouting from her office. After I told her what happened, she took all three men to a meeting room. We could still hear Mr. Bitter ranting, even with the door closed. I quickly wrapped up our team meeting and headed back to my desk.

I looked at the time. It was only 10:05 a.m.

Who cares if someone vandalized my coffee maker or some fuming manager griped about the project we've sweated over for weeks, I thought, trying to calm myself.

*It's not like I slipped on a banana peel in front of my crush.
Silver linings, Dasia, silver linings!*

I touched the branches of my bonsai tree. "What's going on? If you know anything, you should tell me."

Water.

I needed water to soothe my throat, which felt like sandpaper.

I sprinted to the water dispenser, but just as I reached it, searing pain shot through my leg, and I screamed in agony. I'd twisted my right ankle, just like that.

I took off my heels and returned to my desk barefoot. After putting on flats, I hobbled to the bathroom as tears began to flow like a waterfall in spring.

I'm not sure if I'm sobbing due to emotional hysteria or physical pain, but here I am trying to get myself to stop.

Sarah knocks harder on the door.

"I'll be out in a few minutes, promise," I say, tremblingly.

"Okay, love, I'll be waiting in my office."

So much has transpired in the last twenty-four hours, and now my ankle has joined the party.

I totter into Sarah's office. Each time I shift my weight, a sharp jolt of agony shoots up my leg, leaving me gasping for air.

She looks taken aback. "Oh, darling, what now?"

"I know. It's one of those 'what now?' days."

"I don't mean that, Dasia. Why are you limping?"

"I twisted my ankle." I take a deep breath. "But I need to talk to you about something else."

230

She looks at my ankle. The skin around the area is already turning red, and I can feel the swelling. Sarah grabs her purse. "We're going to the nearest urgent-care center. You may have done more than twist it."

I am with Sarah in the waiting room. I feel as if the pain in my ankle must be messing with my brain cells because I also see Luke. I can't believe my eyes, but here he is. A smile creeps onto my face despite my efforts to keep it at bay. I know I shouldn't feel this way, but the man has a way of making me smile.

"How're you holding up?" he asks, sounding concerned. "Charlene said you hurt your ankle."

My mind struggles to justify the warmth that engulfs me. *Danger!* it reminds me.

I suddenly cry out as pain explodes through my leg, leaving me trembling in anguish.

Luke sprints to get help, his voice loud with worry. "She's in agony! Can we get someone over here?"

A few hours later, I'm lying in a bed at the urgent-care center, and Sarah is holding my hand. The pain medication is doing its job.

"You'll go home shortly," she says. "I'll get a cab for you. But the doctor says the recovery may take several weeks."

I groan. I don't have time for a long recovery.

I stretched some ligaments but nothing is broken,

which is a relief. My ankle is wrapped, no crutches needed.

Soon, Sarah helps me get into a cab, and when it reaches my building, the driver helps me get out. I thank her and tip her generously.

As I swing open the main door of my building, I blink at the sight of the stairs. I didn't think of those. Although it's only one flight, there's no way that I can put pressure on my ankle. So I sit on the first step and call Jay, hoping he's returned from Birmingham.

No answer.

I feel lost, hopeless, and desperate. I vow to hunt down whoever propagated the falsehood that "happiness is a mere choice" and start a campaign against their deceitful statement.

Taking a deep breath, I put my purse in my lap, sit on the bottom step, place my hands behind me, and scooch myself up a step with the help of my left foot.

Woo-hoo! It works!

I repeat the crablike motion several times, taking small breaks between scooching and pushing. Finally, I reach the top of the stairs. I feel weightless when I stand and then lumber with heaviness toward my flat.

The sound of the key in the lock is music to my ears. I turn it. There's no movement. Furrowing my brow, I move the key upwards, downwards, sideways. I pull and push the door. All to no avail. Finally, I slide to the floor and rest my head against the wall. I have nothing more to offer the day.

I see my mother sitting underneath a giant oak tree wearing a stunning white dress. She looks entrancing. Each of her eyes is a different color. The tree's branches spread from one side of the earth to another. A little girl is blossoming on a branch, dangling her legs, giggling. My mother reaches for her and then turns briskly when she hears another sweet voice coming from a different tree branch. A little boy is dangling his legs, too, chuckling.

She touches my shoulder. "Dasia, Dasia!"

But her voice sounds different.

I blink once, and again. When my eyes focus, I see Jay studying my face. He's gently shaking my shoulder.

"Are you okay, lovey? Why are you dozing in the hallway?"

"I wanted to experiment with sleeping in the hallway to avoid your snoring," I say sarcastically.

"The mockery tells me you're okay. Let's take you inside. But, uh . . . What on earth did you do to your leg?"

I wave away his question and hold his hands as I stand up.

"Sorry, I was in the shower and missed your call," he says, guiding me inside. "When I called back, I could hear your ringtone outside our front door. Imagine my confusion. Why didn't you come in?"

I lie down on the couch. "I couldn't unlock the door. I think your key was in the lock, blocking mine from the inside."

He covers his face with both hands. "I'm really sorry."

He walks toward the kitchen. "Let me make you a warm herbal tea, and we'll talk."

"Yeah, herbal tea, but no talk, please."

"Sure."

I close my eyes, hoping to see my mother and the oak tree and the giggling little girl and chuckling small boy again.

Nothing appears.

Chapter Thirty-One

I haven't moved from the couch since I got home, and Jay is cooking what smells like a delicious dinner.

I see my phone flashing and swiftly answer the call.

"Hi, Sarah."

"Guess what? It was Luke's girlfriend from the HR department. I'm furious!"

"Who was . . . What was Luke's . . . What are you saying, Sarah?"

"Luke confronted her today. Emilia is the one who destroyed your stuff. I can't talk much now, I must dash, but I'll tell you everything tomorrow. You're not coming to work until you feel better. I'll call you over the weekend."

"Okay, Sarah, speak soon."

Luke's girlfriend. A damning phrase. Bitterness hits me like a ton of bricks. So, Luke and Emilia are dating, and she ravaged my coffee machine. But why?

"The girlfriend," I murmur out loud.

My mind struggles to process this information, while my heart reacts in a way I don't understand. Why this overwhelming feeling of melancholy? I need Jay to help me analyze the facts.

I get up so fast that I see tiny stars and then hobble into the kitchen.

"Jay! Luke has a girlfriend, and she's the one who destroyed my coffee station."

I've never seen Jay's jaw drop this low, have never seen his eyes this wide. He appears to be speechless. His expression is hilarious. Overwhelmed by a surge of laughter, I collapse into a nearby chair, tears streaming down my face. Tears of emotion join my tears of laughter.

Jay puts a hand on my arm. "Can we start over? What do you mean, someone damaged your coffee station?"

It suddenly occurs to me that I haven't told Jay anything about my week. "Uh-huh. I'll start from the beginning," I say, making myself comfortable in the chair.

He continues preparing dinner as I speak, and many minutes later, I conclude my recap. "And then you found me by our door."

Jay comes over and wraps his arms around me. "Oh, darling. What a terrible day."

"Not over yet! Hold tight, my friend. Can you bring my purse from my bedroom?" He does that swiftly. I take out the note from my purse, "I found this note from a wannabe villain."

I hand it to him.

"Whoa whoa whoa. These letters are cut from magazines. It looks like your villain couldn't decide on a font."

I chuckle.

"But, why is this in your handbag?" he asks, a question that seems logical given the circumstances. With a sigh, I simply shrug my shoulders, for nothing seems to make sense anymore, not even my own actions.

"Did you find a follow-up note?"

"Nope." I shake my head.

"I have your red stapler. Bring three reams of printing paper and a dozen highlighters to the copy room if you ever want to see it again."

I know he's trying to make me laugh, but the idea of a follow-up note frightens me. It must show on my face.

"Oh, my darling Dasia." He sits next to me. "Sorry, I was just trying to lift your spirits. This is serious. It's severe. Did you report it?"

"I didn't. So much happened afterward that it slipped my mind. But why would Luke's girlfriend vandalize my things, Jay? And it must be her too, the note?"

He smiles. "What's remarkable is how oblivious you are, Dasia. She knew before you or Luke that you two have the hots for each other."

I don't say anything.

"As Shakespeare said, 'Thee will I love, and with thee lead my life.'"

"Jay, please talk to me in simple language." I put my hands on either side of my head and then move them outward, pretending to expand my head's size. "And I do not have the hots for him," I say, my voice rising.

"Okay, girl, whatever you say. I suppose it takes forever for some people to figure it out." He gestures for me to start eating the delicious-smelling, gorgeous-looking dinner. "And what now?"

"I don't know," I say, scooping ravioli onto my plate. "Sarah was in a rush. She just told me that Luke confronted his girlfriend, and I guess she admitted it was her. I don't know the rest of the story. I'm not going to call Luke, and I don't want to disturb Sarah. I'll find out more when she calls me."

"That woman must face the consequences of her actions."

"Well, she must have been pretty upset to do something like this."

"I don't care how upset she was, Dasia—her actions are unacceptable."

"Yes, of course. She wanted to upset me, and she succeeded. But ultimately, she had no reason whatsoever. Luke and I are not a thing." I pause, thinking. "She was always asking me about Luke."

"Of course she was asking about Luke. Are you surprised?"

"I suppose not. But don't you think one incident shouldn't define a whole person?"

"Too philosophical, Dasia. Too deep right now. I'm defining her by what she's done. She made choices."

I study Jay for a few seconds. "You're right, of course.

"

I take a bite of the cheesy ravioli, and blissful flavors burst in my mouth. "I never thought ravioli could blow my mind. Compliments to the chef."

Jay stands, spreads his arms, flaps his wrists, and bows. I laugh, and then I laugh harder when he crumples to the ground.

I think of my day, how it started and how it ended. Battle armor, fear, vandalism, physical pain, compassion, tears, disappointment, friendship, hope, and laughter. All within a day. How much accumulates in a lifetime?

I think of the times I tripped in life, the times I made wrong judgments and huge mistakes. I can forgive Luke's girlfriend, but what Luke has done is a million times worse. He keeps too much hidden.

It looks as if Emilia knows my past and my secret. She must be the one who left the note. My time on this contract is up, unmistakably over.

"Some pudding?" Jay asks, when we finish eating.

"I don't like pudding."

"But you don't even know what pudding I have."

"You just said *pudding,* and I don't like pudding."

Jay looks confused.

"I'm teasing you, Jay," I say with a grin. "When I first moved here, I declined the offers of pudding for months, as I don't like what people in the States refer to as pudding. One night when I was at a pub, my server presented a pudding menu, and I was shocked to see the list of different desserts."

"So, you thought pudding was a specific type of dessert? That's hilarious." Jay chuckles, while serving our desserts. "We're indulging in a delightful treat of home baked Apple Crumble and Custard. That is home-baked, not home-made."

"Looks delicious." I exclaim taking in the sweet aroma in front of me. I clear my throat. "Jay . . ."

"Yes, Sparkles."

"I'm a computer-science engineer. An award winning one." I blurt out, as if adding another layer of strangeness to the madness that surrounded into the week. However, amid the chaos, Jay's friendship gives me the courage to be my true self. I look at him intently, hoping that he won't change his perception of me now that he has this new piece of information.

"And I'm an astrobiologist, nice meeting you." He titters.

I keep my eyes on Jay as he takes a spoonful of his dessert. He pauses before removing the spoon from his mouth. His eyes meet mine, and his pupils grow wider.

"Good gravy!" he roars.

I press my lips together.

"What the . . . ! Yeah, course you are, you little minx."

Jay hasn't stopped staring, and I'm terrified. I'll do anything to keep him in my life. I'll let him know that my past blunders have changed me. That I'm a good friend.

He just kind of sits there for a bit. Then he says, "Wowza, Dasia!" His eyes are illuminated like bright stars in a clear night sky.

"All your little ideas about digitalizing my art. The app that you suggested. Oh man. CalliPal. You developed that app, didn't you?"

I nod. "It's not a big deal. Making an app is actually easy for me."

"Wow! But why are you hiding all this?" The curiosity in his eyes interrupts my heartbeats.

"Are you upset with me?" I ask.

"None of us are without some fault to hide. But I don't understand."

"I'll tell you the whole story, Jay. I made huge mistakes. But please give me a little time."

He locks his eyes on me. "I may not share your views or approve of your past actions, but you're still my fabulous friend. Please remember that."

My heart melts. The dark-brown pools of his eyes are surrounded by faint halos of lighter specks. It's almost as if two shining circles are linked to his soul, radiating peace toward me.

He continues. "Think of the word *mistake*. Sometimes, we 'miss the take.' That's okay. We just figure out how to get it right next time. Take all the time you need. I care about you for who you are to me. I even love you just the way you are." He winks, and I cackle.

"Unconditionally?" I ask.

"Unconditionally, Sparkles."

I take it easy over the weekend and on Monday, I'm in my living room booting up my company laptop. I'm wearing makeup, a white dress shirt, and a pair of wide-leg sweatpants. My right leg is resting on an ottoman. The top half of me is all business, and my bottom half is dressed for lounging at home. As if I didn't have enough disparity in my life.

I'll work from home for a few days, until I can put weight on my ankle again. Last night was challenging. I had strange dreams and a throbbing ankle drumming pain into my leg.

I was woken by a call from Sarah. "Hope this isn't too early, Dasia. I know you get up early."

"Not at all, Sarah," I said, stretching my left arm over my head in bed.

She told me that a company laptop was on its way to me and that I should call the IT department to set it up.

"Do you have any more news about the incident?" I blurted, once she finished as we didn't have a chance to speak over the weekend.

"Yes. It's all being taken care of by the HR department. I'll give you a detailed update when we get together. I need to rush into a meeting now. Is that okay?"

"Of course," I said, grappling with the unease that contradicted my words.

Jay and I arranged our living room into a work environment that includes a neat corner where I can take video calls and attend meetings.

Now, my laptop is ready, and I check my calendar. I

have two meetings to attend. One is the morning huddle—I'll ask a project member to lead. The other is a project meeting that Luke is chairing.

My breath becomes shallow. I think of my bonsai tree, the note, the pictures in the hidden drawer, and my coffee machine. I feel vulnerable and violated. My thoughts are disorganized: *Luke has an ill-mannered girlfriend. Luke has a brutal girlfriend. Luke has a vicious girlfriend. Luke has a girlfriend.*

"Life happens," I say aloud. "Coffee helps."

I wish I could transport Pages and Beans into our living room—and Roy with it. He called on Saturday to see how I was doing. His friendship is becoming a bright spot in my life, and I'm grateful for it.

I limp into the kitchen and make two cups of Turkish coffee. I leave one in the kitchen for Jay and carry another into the living room in the cutest small coffee cup, which is a delight to hold.

I settle back into my seat and raise my leg onto the ottoman, huffing and puffing. I inhale deeply, taking in the huge coffee scent from the tiny coffee cup. The aroma is deep and sweet. Then I click the remote-access link to join the project meeting.

Luke is in his crisp light-blue shirt; his jacket hangs on his chair. My blood boils. I note his stubble and hope that he gives his girlfriend a beard burn.

He checks to see if everyone attending virtually can be seen and heard. I'm hoping for some explanation from him, some acknowledgment, such as, "My girlfriend vandalized your personal belongings, I'm so sorry, yadda yadda yadda."

But Luke starts the meeting with an announcement. "We have to scrap the meeting agenda as we have a serious cybersecurity breach. We received an anonymous email from someone claiming to have accessed patient data—specific data that we collected as part of the project. They want us to pay a ransom."

I stare, openmouthed. We all do.

"What type of data?" someone asks.

"Everything—addresses, dates of birth, medical records."

"How is this even possible?" I ask.

"We're looking into it. Our cybersecurity team suggested that maybe we failed to follow certain protocols, or maybe a user downloaded sensitive information to a local device, which can't be encrypted. Or it could be an issue with a vulnerable remote network."

Sarah holds her head in her hands. "Oh! This is absolutely dreadful. Can you imagine if they use that personal data for their own gain?"

I break into a cold sweat. My breath quickens. I snap off my camera. I can't bear the thought of anyone seeing the fear on my face. I cover my mouth and my shoulders tense up.

Did I cause this?

Was it the result of my fixing the integration issues?

Or downloading the file from Luke's computer?

The possibilities buzz in my mind like irate bees.

I can hear my mother's voice: *See what you've done!* It meshes with Sarah's: "Are you there?"

"Dasia, are you there?" asks Luke.

I swallow, sit straight, and remind myself to blink. Finally, I turn on my camera again. "Yes, I'm sorry. My ankle was playing up."

"Are you okay now?"

"I am, thank you," I manage to utter through gritted teeth, but the truth is, I'm light-years away from being okay.

"How bad is this?" I ask.

"Okay, so, patient data in the wrong hands is bad news," says Sarah. "Financial scams, targeting of vulnerable people, fraud, identity theft—you name it."

"I have an urgent meeting now with the cybersecurity team," says Luke. "I have to go." He disappears.

I tap my left foot fiercely. I bite my lip. I should offer to help, whether I caused this breach or not. My interventions likely weakened cybersecurity. I could help them catch the hackers and stop them from hurting people. I need to call Luke and ask for an urgent meeting with him and Sarah.

I pull up Luke's contact info on my phone, but my hand quakes so violently that I throw the device to the other side of the living room. I open my mouth to wail, but no sound comes out. Instead, I hear a strange noise, like a toy voice talking at a distance.

"Hello, hello?"

I look around and realize that it's coming from my

phone. Darn, I must have dialed Luke's number when I threw the phone. I take my right leg into my hands, put it down, and then drag myself to the phone.

"Hello."

"Hello, Dasia. You called me but then disappeared."

"By mistake," I say, freezing up. "I didn't mean to call you."

"Ah, okay then," he says, and hangs up.

"Darn, darn, darn," I say out loud.

I call back.

"Is this another pocket-dial? Lock your phone, Dasia."

"Uh-uh. Luke . . . I might have an idea how to catch those hackers."

"Is that so now?" He doesn't sound surprised. "Do whatever you can to stop them, Dasia."

"Do you mean that?"

"Yes. We need to stop them. Do whatever you can."

And he's gone.

I get on my computer and remain glued to the screen for hours, eating my meals in the same spot. As the day wears on into the night, I keep working. And just before midnight, I yell with excitement.

"Here's a selection of excellent cheeses! Come and get it, you conniving, treacherous, deceitful, devious, deceptive, criminal wretches."

It's going to be a long night, as I'm determined to stay up and watch their every move. Zero diversions, zero downtime. I'll be their shadow, silently observing.

Chapter Thirty-Two

I created a decoy system using data and applications as bait. It's a combination of computer science, reverse engineering, and traditional detective work. The bait is like cheese—Gouda, Manchego, feta, and some aged cheddar. They'll think these are legitimate targets, and when they attack, I can gather information on who they are. Mouse and cheese.

Since midnight, I've had my eyes on the screen, hoping to see activity, but nothing has happened yet. It's almost 8 a.m. on Tuesday morning.

I receive a text message. Luke.

> Good morning, Dasia. Will you video-call me when you can?

I call him immediately, and his face appears on the screen.

"Hey, how are you feeling?"

"I'm much better, thank you."

I want to update him on my hacker-catching work, but he continues. "Listen, we now know who damaged your coffee maker, and the person has been suspended. We'll update you when you return to the office."

I nod, although I already know it's his girlfriend. *I guess he's not letting me in on that detail*, I think, mentally rolling my eyes.

"Okay, and another thing—we have a huge problem, Dasia. Yesterday's hacking situation escalated. Can you join a meeting in five?"

"Of course." A sense of uneasiness grips me. What could be worse than what we already face? *One disaster at a time*, I tell myself, while I dial in.

When I connect, I see Sarah and Tanya,the cybersecurity lead, arriving in the meeting room. Sarah is visibly distressed, and Tanya looks depleted.

"This is a nightmare!" Sarah says. "The hackers are now demanding a whopping half a million, threatening to sell the data on the dark web, lock us out of our systems, and even block access to medical records." She looks as though she's about to jump out of a plane without a parachute.

"The hackers have gotten hold of diagnostic records, elective-surgery records—some of these patients might be in the middle of an operation. These are people with serious medical needs. The hackers surely can't block our access, can they?"

Her words send a shiver of dread through me.

"Most probably they're bluffing," says Tanya. "Accessing data is one thing; blocking our access is something else."

I think of the clinicians not being able to access patient records when they need them the most. "They might be bluffing, but it's always better to overestimate their skills," I say. "They can see the computers and files as we see them. So, yes, it's possible that they can do everything that they threaten to do. But there are ways to catch them in the act."

At this point, I couldn't care less about my secret, my background, or who knows what. But no one seems to notice that my comments are way above my pay grade.

"How do we catch them in the act, Dasia?" Luke asks, but Tanya raises her voice before I can respond.

"We need to shut down all the servers until we can examine all the stations for the malware."

Sarah looks even more distressed. "But we have thousands of patients with urgent needs. We can't just shut down all the servers."

Then I hear Mr. Goodwin's voice. It rumbles like a tsunami of ice crashing into the office walls. "What the hell is going on here?" he says, barging into the meeting room. I'm relieved I'm not there in person.

"It all began with this automation project!" he shouts. "We should have just laid people off. I should have gone with my gut feeling. The board will be livid. This is nothing short of a complete and utter disaster." He glowers. "Do something to find these lowlifes or else you'll all have to find other jobs." With that, he storms out of the room.

Luke carries on as if Mr. Goodwin didn't interrupt our meeting. "We have less than twelve. We have to act fast." He sounds as if he carries the weight of the entire planet on his shoulders.

As soon as I disconnect, I call a taxi and rush to get ready. My ankle hurts, but I don't care. I'll ignore the throbbing. I put on a pair of dark trousers with wide legs and a light-green sweater and grab my purse. The vast blue sky envelopes me as I step out of my building, but the heaviness of the situation bears down on my chest.

So here's your reward, Dasia, for taking risks and leaping.

When I arrive at the office, I hear voices. And I hear the ticking of a bomb in my eardrums.

Sarah sees me and looks at my ankle with worry.

"I'm okay," I say.

"Luke went to the hospital site with Tanya," she explains.

I settle in and start watching the traps again. My eyelids are red and itchy with lack of sleep. Minutes later, Luke calls, and Sarah puts him on speakerphone.

"So, Luke, you know I mentioned that I had an idea," I say, "and you told me to do whatever I can to catch the hackers."

"Uh-huh . . . Did I? Yes, I did. I'm on my way back, not far from the office now."

I feel a crushing pressure seize my being and slowly

make its way to my throat from every direction. I hold on to the edge of the desk to support my trembling legs.

"I created a pretty good dummy application to catch the hackers in the act. I've just sent a detailed email to Tanya and copied both of you."

"You did what?" Sarah's voice is unrecognizable.

"I hope no one gets harmed, Dasia," says Luke.

I hope no one gets harmed. I hope no one gets harmed. I hope no one gets harmed.

The words ring in my head like a death knell. It's the most terrifying sentence I've ever heard. I think of the patients, vulnerable people whose personal information might be in the hands of malicious criminals.

Sarah looks at me, and I can't read her expression.

"Give me a few moments, please." I need oxygen, so I step out of the office, my ankle pounding with each step.

I look to the sky, but no sky exists. All I see is a big dark hole.

It's 11 a.m. I'm standing by the river, leaning against its wall. A howl expands in my chest. I open my mouth, but the silence is deafening.

There's been a crash.

Voices from both the past and the present play relentlessly in my mind, refusing to quiet down.

251

I hope no one was hurt, *Dasia*, says my former assistant software engineer.

I hope no one gets harmed, barks my current boss.

How is it that the words spoken years apart are nearly identical and equally terrifying? It's as if I'm trapped in some sort of dizzying, never-ending vortex where the past and present swirl around me. The ground beneath my feet seems to vanish into thin air. I grasp the railing on the wall to steady myself.

I squeeze my eyes shut, desperate to stop the tears from spilling down my cheeks, but they flow relentlessly. My mind races with a thousand different thoughts, all jumbled together in a tangled mess of fear and uncertainty. Did I make a mistake that could have catastrophic consequences?

A sudden resolve takes hold of me.

I stand tall. As I inhale deeply, filling my lungs with fresh air, my rib cage welcomes the expansion, allowing me to stand even taller.

I wipe off the tears. I can't change what has already happened, but I can control how I react to it. I can face whatever happens next. My inner thoughts urge me to stop crying and move forward. I take a deep, shuddering breath, steeling myself for the difficult task ahead. The clock is ticking, but I'll not let the pressure break me. I will catch those responsible for the terrible act.

I gaze up at the towering office building before me and formulate my next steps. Finally, feeling calmer, I turn to the river for a beat before starting to walk back to the office.

I gasp as something sharp presses into the right side of my waist. I shift my body to ease the pain, but it just intensifies. What is this?

I turn my head and see Emilia. Then my gaze falls to where I feel the pain. I see the cold metal blades of the scissors she holds. She's pushing the tips into my side.

"What are you doing?" I cry, unable to move.

"Things were all good until you had to show up and ruin everything for me." Her eyes are narrowed in a sharp glare.

"What?" I ask, reeling from pain and confusion.

"You're a curse," she hisses through gritted teeth.

Well, at least we agree on something.

I understand the sorrow beneath the fury in her eyes. It's a look that says, "I lost everything." This is a woman who is broken into thousands of pieces.

"You're hurting me," I whisper, wincing.

She remains still.

I have less than nine hours to catch the hackers.

"Please, Emilia, I don't know what you're talking about." I look around desperately, but no one notices us. I try to talk sense into her.

"I won't tell anyone, I promise. Just let me go."

She doesn't budge. I'm wedged between the scissors and the river wall. I can hear her heavy breath, can feel her eyes drilling into me like a chisel into stone.

"I know you secretly go into Luke's office, peeking around," she utters, seething.

"Oh . . . that's what your note was about," I say. It hadn't been about my secret after all. "I was searching for something for the board meeting. Luke gave me permission to be in his office." My voice trembles with desperation. "Emilia, there are patients in danger. We have less than nine hours to help them. You need to let me go."

"What do you mean *danger*?" She eases the pressure on the scissors a little.

"Emilia!"

Luke's voice reaches my ears like an enormous ocean wave crashing onto rocky cliffs. The pain in my side disappears as Emilia turns and hides the scissors behind her back.

Luke is sprinting toward us. "What's going on?" he shouts, out of breath.

"Nothing, Luke," I say, trying to calm my heavy breathing. Emilia locks her eyes with mine; the intensity makes me shudder.

She suddenly takes off, and we both watch her disappear into the busy streets of London.

Luke rests both hands on my shoulders. "Are you okay?"

I force myself not to wince as pain shoots through my right side. Internally, I feel a sense of relief at the sight of him.

"Everything's okay," I say, avoiding his eyes and looking down.

"Dasia! You're shaken." He pulls me into his arms, and I rest my head on his shoulder, touching the hole in my green sweater.

I find myself in a tug-of-war. My mind urges me to step back and resist the comfort of his embrace. He's not to be trusted. But my heart urges me closer, reminding me of his kindness, care, and charm. Finally, my physical being makes the decision to fully indulge in his strong arms.

I allow myself only a minute of comfort. Then I take a step back.

"She dug a pair of scissors into my side!" I blurt, my voice trembling with a mix of shock and fear.

The words hang heavy in the air.

Luke's pupils dilate, expanding like a vast universe before me. "What? Where? Are you hurt?" Then his face contorts with rage, and a vein in his forehead pulses. He unleashes a torrent of furious shouts and curses.

I silence him by pressing my hand against his mouth. "Luke, listen. We need to get back to work and apprehend those hackers," I whisper urgently. "We have less than nine hours."

Chapter Thirty-Three

I t's 2:00 p.m.

My eyes are glued to the screen, watching for activity. We have six hours. I look up and see Luke standing by my desk. My eyes are even itchier than before. His eyelids are heavy and his eyes are sad, as if a storm cloud has taken them over.

He sits in the chair in front of my desk. Perhaps he finally wants to come clean about the photos in his drawer. "How's it going?"

"I'll get them, Luke," I say, despite the tiny skeptical voice inside me.

"Can I ask you a question?"

"Sure, but I can't take my eyes off the screen."

"Why did you leave your home and never return, Dasia?"

"What?" I say, taken aback by his question.

I glance at him, and he seems troubled. His brow is furrowed.

"Let me guess," he says. "You either left a man at the altar, embezzled millions from your work, or killed someone."

"Maybe a combination of all three," I say, but I'm not in the mood for games.

He sets a printout of a news article on my desk. "How about this?"

I look at the paper and my heart thumps rapidly. The article is about the accident. The one I was responsible for. The one that caused hospitalizations and a coma that lasted three months and three days. The one that knocked my ex-husband off his feet. The one that made my dad's heart give out.

I'm plunged into an ocean of despair.

"Where did you get this?"

Luke shakes his head. "Emilia emailed it to me yesterday, but I only saw it today. Just printed a copy."

Emilia again.

"We've less than six hours, Luke."

"I know, Dasia," he says firmly. I can feel him staring at me intensely "It all makes sense now. Let's talk for a few minutes. Please."

He stresses the word *please*, as if to emphasize that it's an invitation and not a demand. I grab the laptop and keep my eyes on the dummy application as we walk to his office. Each step takes an eternity. The world I've constructed is on the verge of crumbling down around me.

As I lower myself onto a chair, the weight of the moment pushes me down. Hard.

"Do you want a glass of water?" he asks, as he sits across from me.

I shake my head. Looking at Luke, I detect no signs of animosity. I feel perplexed.

"Luke, please let me continue helping the cybersecurity team. I'll tell you everything once we catch the hackers. But can I please speak to Sarah first? She deserves to hear it all from me."

"Yes, you'll certainly continue helping. There's no doubt you've already been a big help. I've done some research on you, and I feel more assured about apprehending those hackers now." Then he shifts uncomfortably.

"But . . ." He frowns. "But I don't understand why you've hidden your incredible abilities. Who are you, Dasia?"

"I'll explain—I promise. Let me focus on catching these lowlifes first." I can't look into his eyes.

"Sure," he says, just as Sarah rushes into his office.

Her voice is shaky. "They blocked staff access to the patients' medical records." Her eyes are red, and tears are gathering.

I check the time on my phone. "But we still have five hours and thirteen minutes! Did we lose access to patient records now?"

"No, we have the medical records backed up in the system, but there's no way to deliver them to hundreds of doctors, nurses, or anyone who needs them urgently. Patients currently undergoing surgeries could face severe harm. People could die! Oh, my goodness, we didn't think they could do this."

It happened. I couldn't catch them, and as a result, more people will come to harm because of me.

"We lost the battle. This also means they can do whatever they want with the personal information. Oh my . . ." Sarah says, before collapsing into a chair.

A haunting, eerie silence descends on the room. My head is spinning, and my stomach is making funny sounds.

We lost it. I lost again.

I press my teeth hard into my lip, feeling a sharp pinch and tasting a metallic tang.

I bring the back of my hand to my mouth, smearing the blood.

Fear washes over me, and a bolt of pain shoots through my body.

I hurt people, and I may have killed people.

I did it again.

I sprint out of Luke's office without my purse or phone. My ankle is throbbing, but I don't slow down. As I get into the elevator, I hear Luke and Sarah calling my name, but it's too late. Sarah is better off without me. When the elevator lets me off in the lobby, I run into the street without a direction or purpose.

I don't know how long I run. My lungs are burning, I have a sharp pain in my lower belly. My ankle finally gives out. I can't carry my body anymore. I stop, stand on one leg, and look around. I'm by the river. I move to the wall, lean over it, and weep.

I'm in one of the busiest parts of London, the South Bank. I hear some people asking me if I'm okay, and I dismiss them with a wave. *No, I'm not*, but no one can do anything about it.

I stop sobbing, but the tears continue. I stumble to a bench and sit.

I failed to fix it. I caused more harm.

Pulling up my knees, I rest my head on them. Moments later, I feel a hand on my shoulder.

"Having a bad day, love?"

I nod without taking my head off my knees.

"Can I get you water or anything else from that café?" the stranger asks.

"Water, please," I mumble.

The woman leaves and then returns a few minutes later. I hear her place a paper bag next to me. "Here it is," she says. "I promise things will get better."

I peer into the bag—there's a small bottle of water, some tissues, a banana, and a bar of chocolate, along with a twenty-pound note. I look up to thank her, but she's gone.

I notice that the sky is deep blue, like my brother's eyes. I open the glossy wrapper on the chocolate bar and snap off a piece. The sound makes me jump. I take a bite.

"Seven Hells," I murmur, as all my emotions flood into my taste buds.

Tears start again, and then I hear someone call my name. Suddenly, I feel arms enveloping me.

"Dasia, hey, hey!"

I wipe the tears with the back of my arm. My mother hated that.

"Roy," I whisper. "Why? You're here . . . But why?"

"I've been looking for you, running around in a frenzy."

His eyes are intense. I stand up and step back, shaking my head.

"Please, Dasia, let's go somewhere. Things usually feel worse than they really are." His phone rings. "One second," he says, and answers the call. "Yes, I found her. Yeah, she's okay."

I grab the bag. "I need to go now, Roy. I'll be okay."

I run to the Tube, and my whole leg beats with pain all the way home. My waist is also sore from the scissors pressing into my flesh. But nothing hurts as much as my heart.

I'm holding my treasure bag tightly as I turn my key in the lock. I'm relieved to find that Jay isn't home. I can do without him fussing around me right now.

I collapse onto my bed, and regret crawls from my heart into every fiber in my body. I start punching my soft pillow. Then I splash cold water on my face and sit in front of my personal laptop. I can't give up. I'll have to go where no one else will dare to go if I want to catch these cyberninjas. I'll have to use everything I know about digital forensics to help me devise a plan.

I'll have to access the dark web.

It's 5:00 p.m.

I email Tanya to update her, and she responds immediately.

```
These are dangerous individuals. You
should stop and let us deal with
them.
```

I reply,

```
I'll update you regularly. I have to
go now.
```

The dark web is a place for illegal activities and nefarious characters. It has secret underground networks where one can buy credit card info or ransomware data. It's nothing like the web that we normally use.

I navigate the maze of sites and forums and finally find a highly secretive thread about a recent hospital breach. The thread is filled with comments from hackers boasting about their success.

I create a hacker profile with an impressive background. But I have to be careful. The dark web is a place where anonymity is everything, and one wrong move could expose my identity and make me a target of the very hackers I'm trying to catch.

Suddenly, I hear a loud noise outside my window. A loud, jarring noise. My heart pounds like a jackhammer. For a moment, my mind races with all sorts of terrifying scenarios: the hackers somehow found me; they're outside my window, ready to break in.

I slowly regain my composure and force myself to peek out of the window. The noise was just a passing truck, its engine revving loudly.

It's 1:00 a.m.

Finally, my plan has worked. "Got you!" I shout.

The hackers have invited me to join an invite-only server, where I can chat with other hackers. Although these are extremely experienced and dangerous individuals, I feel a bit of excitement. I can't believe I'm doing something illegal, though it's ultimately for a good cause.

Once I join the server, I quickly get to work. I install a hidden keylogger that will allow me to monitor their keystrokes and screen activity. Next, I begin gathering as much information as possible about their operations. The rest is more straightforward—analyzing their digital footprint and their comments on their recent and most successful hacking jobs.

"You think you know it all, you guys? You haven't met *me* yet!" I say, as I start to see patterns and weaknesses in their network.

My heart flips as if it's on a trampoline when I find a trail that will infiltrate their system and let me access their files.

"Well, well, well! It looks like the party is over, girls

and boys! You're one step closer to getting your butts thrown in jail!" I say, smiling what's perhaps my first smile since I created the dummy application.

It's Wednesday, 5:00 a.m.

I haven't slept for almost forty-eight hours.

I send a follow-up email to Tanya, and copy Sarah and Luke.

```
URGENT — I've got them!
```

Tanya replies,

```
Terrific! I'll inform the
authorities. We must leave this in
their hands now.
```

"Ab-so-lute-ly," I mumble, rubbing my bleary eyes.

I see emails from Sarah and Luke—it looks like no one slept tonight. But I don't read them. I only want to talk to my brother, but I left my phone at work. So I send him an email.

Eli,

I'm terrified. I've done it again. I possibly harmed people. I understand if you don't want such a sister in your life.

I slam the laptop shut, feeling a surge of frustration and despair. It's done. I caught them. But the lingering uncertainty nibbles at my conscience. I can't help but wonder if anyone was harmed earlier, or worry about the stress and anguish that this situation has inflicted upon people. I close my eyes, hoping to find solace amidst the chaos.

I either fall asleep or black out, and when I wake up, I gasp for air. I push myself into a sitting position, my sheets twisted around my legs. Cold sweat beads on my forehead and the back of my neck. Morning sun peeks into my room, and I realize that I still haven't heard from Jay, which is surprising.

I don't move from my bed, just stare at the ceiling, then the walls, then the ceiling again. Then I grab the bag beside my bed, the one nice stranger brought me. I haven't eaten in hours. I have a breakfast of half a banana and a few sips of water.

I sit in bed until I finally hear Jay. I step out of my bedroom and into the kitchen. "Hey, good morning!" I say.

Jay doesn't say a word, just walks out of the kitchen with a stone face.

Oh dear. He knows too. He knows what I've done, and he hates me.

With all my mistakes and secrets, I don't deserve close friends. But I desperately want to chase after him, to plead with him to understand that I'm still the same Dasia.

The words won't come.

Instead, I bolt into my bedroom, and the agonizing pain of losing Jay comes crashing through me like a avalanche—overwhelming and unstoppable.

266

Chapter Thirty-Four

A few hours later, I sit in bed in disbelief. I'm hugging my laptop tight. Eli's booked a flight to London. He hates flying. He doesn't fly. He even once drove from one coast of the country to the other to attend his best friend's wedding.

I read your email just before midnight and booked a flight taking off at 6:00 a.m. I'll be heading to the airport shortly and expect to arrive in the evening, UK time. Don't try to persuade me otherwise, sis, as I'm feeling brave. I've been watching videos on "how to fly without fear." Save your energy for other things, like showing me around London, just as you've always wanted to. See you in a few hours.

    Love,

    Eli

He'll arrive this evening. Having dozed for only a few hours, I still feel sleep-deprived; I have no energy.

I strain to hear Jay in the flat. Suddenly, I bolt upright.

"Fight for your friend," I declare out loud.

I feel like a hot mess. My hair is sticking to my face, and I'm certain I have puffy eyes and a red nose. I knock on Jay's door, hard and loud. He swings it open but wears the same stone face I saw earlier.

"What?"

"Don't 'what' me!" I say, fueled by my love of our friendship. "Let me try to explain, at least."

"What can you even explain? I expected you to respect me."

"But, I wanted to tell you, Jay. I just couldn't make myself. I made a mistake. Remember those two words? *Miss* and *take*," I say, attempting to get through to him.

"I'm disappointed and angry with you. And don't bat those eyelashes; your teary hazel eyes won't work either."

I messed up.

"Can I try a begging face, please?" I gaze down and clasp my hands in front of my face.

His expression softens a little. But only for a moment. "This isn't a joke, Dasia."

Oh goodness, I lost him.

"Jay, I want to apologize for not being completely honest with you and keeping a secret. I never intended to hurt anyone."

He looks away, taking in my words. "Yes, I'm hurt," he says, softening a little again.

"I'm sorry. I'm struggling to come to terms with my actions, and trust me, I'm filled with self-loathing. I haven't gone near any software work since the incident. Well, until recently. And that's only because there were the hackers and I had to intervene." I lean against the wall, feeling weak. "I didn't tell you because I was scared of losing you," I whisper, looking at the ground.

My heart shatters into a million pieces, and I can barely contain my devastation.

"I'll move out," I continue, "but please, give me some time. My brother will be here this evening. Can we stay tonight while I pack my things to move into a hotel?"

He doesn't say a word. I look up and see no anger on his face. Instead, he seems stunned. Finally, he says, "What on earth are you talking about?"

"Huh?"

"Come again? Hackers? Secrets? Mistakes? Are we in a Mission Impossible movie or something?"

"I wish we were!" I pause. "Wait, why are you upset with me?"

"Because you contacted Jarrett behind my back. I bumped into him at a friend's gathering, and he told me that you kinda told him off. He said I should do my dirty work rather than sending a pretty-faced friend."

Oh.

"I'm sorry. That was months ago, when you first told me about him. I was so furious that I couldn't stop myself from searching for him on social media, and then I wrote the message and pressed send before I really thought about it. I know I shouldn't have done that, but I couldn't help it! I hate hearing about anyone hurting you."

I look at him with a guilty expression, and he tilts his head with amusement.

"And now you hate me." My voice trails off as I look at the ground again.

"I don't hate you, but I hate what you did. Two different things, Dasia." I look at him with hope. He sighs. "I'm knackered. Let's take a break and reconvene in a bit. And I need a strong coffee."

"Sure," I say. "I'll brew us some."

"Hey, Sparkles!" he calls, before closing his bedroom door. I turn around with wide eyes. "You don't just give up or stop loving people when they make mistakes. It's easy to be a fair-weather friend, but neither of us fits that mold. So I suppose I should thank you for taking the risk and standing up for me." He smiles, and warmth spreads through me.

As I make my way toward the bedroom, he calls out again, his voice sharper this time. "By the way, you're not moving out. Your brother stays here with us. But you shouldn't have interfered, and I'm still mad at you!"

My face erupts into a grin. This is the best telling-off I've ever heard. Life is simply better with a brilliant friend in it.

Chapter Thirty-Five

"Do you remember how Dad always found a good excuse to take us to our favorite ice cream shop?" asks Eli, sitting on the edge of my bed.

I smile. "Then I'd spoil it by insisting on popping into the library."

He rolls his eyes. "Yes, the science section. How could I forget."

Eli got here earlier this evening, and in the hours leading up to his arrival, I found myself getting excited, counting down the minutes.

"Jay is such a cool friend," he says.

"I know. I'm so lucky."

"I think he knows he's also very lucky to have you as his friend."

"I'm not entirely sure," I say sadly. "I did upset him."

He sighs. "I wish you'd stop working so hard to impress people who already love you, sis."

"I wasn't trying to impress Jay," I clarify. "I shouldn't have contacted his friend."

He grins. "You're a wicked friend and sister."

Both of us startle at the sudden appearance of Jay. "Can you guys meet me in the kitchen?" he asks, before disappearing as quickly as he appeared.

I rush into the bathroom and splash cold water on my face. When I look in the mirror, I see a tired face. I think of Sarah's tired face.

She insisted on a video-call a few hours ago, and I'm glad I agreed to it. I needed to see those caring eyes.

"Dasia, you're extraordinary," she said. "I stayed in the office last night, Luke and Tanya too, waiting for your email to come through. It was risky, but I knew you'd do it. And you did it! The hackers were apprehended and the crisis has been averted. Nobody was hurt. Thankfully, surgeries are routinely done in the morning, so no patient was on an operating table when events unfolded in the afternoon."

Sarah's words dissolved the heavy weight on my chest, and I wiped away the tears brought on by the tide of emotions.

Now, I'm feeling elated.

I head to the kitchen, where Jay's eyes are sparkling. Whatever he has to share with us is something he's very excited about. His excitement is infectious, and I hold my brother's hand, waiting for the reveal.

"Jarrett and I agreed to meet soon."

"Oh. My. Goodness," I say.

"Who's Jarrett?" my brother asks.

"Order, order!" Jay says. "Not done yet! He called, and we argued a bit. Then we decided to meet to talk things out. But he has one condition—and I agreed to it."

I'm all ears. Jay is quiet for a moment, watching me. "We both want you to be there."

I frown. "Who, me? You want me to be there?"

"Yes, you, Dasia. We decided you should be there to experience the uncomfortable atmosphere that's sure to arise."

Eli chuckles.

"If you don't stop that charming chuckle, Mr. America, you'll be ordered to come along too!" Jay says teasingly.

My brother tries to contain his laughter. "Anything for my friend."

I look at my little brother and see a kindhearted man, all grown up.

As morning arrives, both my brother and I feel exhausted since we stayed up until the early hours, talking nonstop.

"Sis, I don't understand why you won't tell the police about how Emilia threated you with scissors."

"She's facing numerous other charges already, and it wasn't as if she always carried a pair of scissors around. I could tell how hurt she was—what good would come from further involving the police? All under the bridge."

"So you're giving her another chance in life?"

"No, I can't do that. It's her call. I'm giving myself another chance; I'd rather move on and start fully living my life at cause."

"At cause?"

"Yes, at cause. My choices create what I want in life. Or what I miss out on. These past few months, and particularly these recent days, have reminded of this truth. It's entirely up to me."

"I'm proud of you," says Eli.

"Anyway, I have no intention of being a part of her life in any way. I choose to move on."

"You know, I wish you could say that about other things in your past. 'All under the bridge.'"

"I'm working on it," I say, shrugging.

He looks at me with affectionate eyes. "That was a mean email. You scared me."

"I know. I'm sorry."

"Why would you send such a bone-chilling email? I wanted to bring a jug of icy water and pour it over your head!"

"I know. No, I don't know. Oh, I'm a mess. And I cannot believe you're sitting here." I pinch his arm, and he shrieks.

"Stop it!"

I can tell something is still bothering him, and I tell him that.

He looks at me with the same admiration he often had when we were growing up. "It's nothing. You gather your strength first."

"Please tell me. What's bothering you?"

"Make me a things-to-do-in-London list, first," he says.

"Don't change the subject, please," I hiss. "Although I love the idea of making a list."

"Do it then. I'm excited to explore this lovely city. But first, I need to sleep for a few hours to overcome this silly jet lag. Want to come with me?"

"Sorry Eli, but I'm exhausted. I need to catch up on rest."

"I can see that," he says, with a mischievous smile.

"Ha ha ha, funny."

Eli leaves in the afternoon, taking with him the London must-do list I had prepared for him.

What's upsetting my little brother? He appears bothered. Is it something to do with Mom? Maybe his love life?

I lie on the couch, feeling my eyelids grow heavy.

Suddenly, I jolt awake, noticing the evening light squeezing through the blinds. No one else is home. Jay volunteered to show my brother around London. Needing more rest to recharge my energy, I gently allow my eyelids to close again.

Jay and Eli return just before 11 p.m., both in a jolly mood. I've been up for a while, watching a Netflix series but not really following the plot, too preoccupied with thoughts about my brother. As soon as they enter, I run from my bedroom into the living room to join their conversation.

"You know your little brother is a beer snob!" Jay says.

"She's only eleven months older than me."

"Okay, not 'little brother,'" Jay says with a smile, before he leaves us for a good night's sleep.

After Eli tells me about his London day, he says, "I'm also ready for a good night's sleep."

Once again, I go to bed wondering what's upsetting my brother and when he'll tell me. But he's happy right now. No need to spoil it.

On Friday evening, the three of us are discussing what to watch. Earlier, we had a nice dinner that Jay cooked for us, and then my brother worked awhile, made some phone calls. Despite only two days passing since his arrival, it already feels as if he has seamlessly become a part of my everyday life.

"Shall we have a chat first, sis?" Eli says.

"I've been waiting for this. Let's go to my bedroom. Bring a chair."

We sit at my small table. "What is it? How can I help my awesome brother?"

"This is about our father." He looks at me. I sit up. "I

know you blame yourself. You think that your incident caused him to have the heart attack. But guess what? Apparently he didn't even know about your incident when he had the heart attack."

A stinging sensation spreads from my heart into every cell of my body—a physical pain.

"What?"

"Yes, sis, he never knew about it. His heart had been acting up for the whole month. Mom didn't tell him about your incident because he wasn't well. So, he didn't know about the accident and that William got into a crash. He had a heart attack and passed away. That's all. Dad's death wasn't your fault and William's accident also isn't your fault—it was his frantic speed."

I'm blazing with fury. "But Mom never said anything!" I roar.

He takes my hand. "It's okay, sis. I'm here."

"When did you find out?" I whisper, my voice escaping me.

"We had a big argument when I booked my flight. She wanted me to convince you to return home. She kept saying that she had things to say to us, and that we needed to be together, at home. Our argument got out of hand, and I told her she was to blame for everything. I told her you were punishing yourself by taking the blame for everyone's tragedies."

"Oh dear . . ."

"Yeah, she stayed in her room until I was getting ready to catch my flight. Finally, she came out, and it looked like she'd aged at least twenty years in a few hours. She gave me this."

He holds out an envelope, and I stare at it for a while.

"Apparently, she wrote this months ago," Eli says.

Both my hands tremble as I take the envelope.

"I'll go and join Jay in the living room. Let me know if you need me." He steps out after placing a kiss on my head.

I move to the window, clenching my fists tighter with every second that passes. Finally, I place the crushed letter on the small table then gingerly take it from its envelope. I feel a knot in my stomach at the sight of her handwriting.

My Dasia,

No matter how hard I tried, you always shone as the gem of this family. I'm sorry for how I treated you all those years, but I just couldn't cope with how much your father favored you.

He was my first love, but I wasn't his first love. I took him away from another woman. Your father was in love with my best friend, Annabel. We all went to the same high school. But I was convinced your father and I should be together. When I found out he planned to propose to her, I did something awful. Something that made your father break up with her. I will not get into the details. Let's just say I was an evil friend, and she was destroyed by the shame and losing your father.

*Then, I got pregnant with you. In those times,
marriage was the only way forward, particularly
because of your dad's family and their background. My
burning desire was to have him look at me the same way
he looked at Annabel. But no matter how hard I tried,
my efforts were in vain—even when I carried you
within me.*

*Then you arrived. His love for you pulsed through
every fiber of his being, his eyes were so intent on you,
they reflected nothing but you. He was so captivated by
you that it seemed that nothing else existed for him.*

*My joy at the birth of my first child was soon
overshadowed by jealousy. No matter how hard I tried,
it was clear that you were your father's entire world,
and I hid my love for you behind a wall of envy. As the
years passed, I kept my heartache buried until it felt like
part of me had died.*

*So, my resentment toward you spiraled out of
control. I began to blame you for his lack of affection.
But it was never you. I suppose when we seek someone
or something to take the blame, oftentimes we look to
the most readily available person—even our own child.*

*I wanted to show him that you weren't the most
perfect little thing in the world, but he was devoted to
you and never doubted how perfect you were. The more I
tried, the shinier you became. Your light was bright and
wonderful until your father died. And I allowed you to
turn off your unique spark. I wanted you to think you
caused his death. It couldn't be further from the truth,*

my girl. He didn't know about the accident. And if he'd known, he would have found a way to comfort and help you.

Over the past few months, I've been in therapy and have come to realize how much pain my personal struggles have caused you.

I also wrote to Annabel, not expecting forgiveness but apologizing for the hurt I caused. To my surprise, she wrote back, asking me to forgive myself and telling me that she has a happy family. She loves her husband and has wonderful kids. She said that the way to heal heartache is with love, and she was pleased to give love another chance after your father broke up with her. She added that she didn't want to hear from me again but would welcome a connection with you, if you wished. And however painful that would be for me, I would respect your decision.

I know how much you love your brother. But I also know that, growing up, you dimmed your light so you wouldn't outshine him.

I've contemplated writing this letter for years. I finally found the courage to write it, but I held on to it, intending to give it to you in person the next time we saw each other.

I'm not asking you to forgive me, but please forgive yourself. You weren't responsible for your dad's death. He didn't know what happened, and if he had, I know he would have supported you unconditionally.

You're much more than who you think you are. I love

you, and overwhelming regret consumes me for never showing you that.

    I am truly and deeply sorry.
    Mom

I stare at the letter as the world I know collapses again. There's a crushing sadness, and I feel as if a strange physical being has taken up residence in my body, heart, and mind. Then, suddenly, I feel numb. I feel nothing whatsoever.

Chapter Thirty Six

As soon as I shut my eyes, I find myself sprinting through the halls of a hospital. In my dream, I can't get a hold of Dad's medical records. Frantically searching, I spot my mother also running.

My eyes snap open. Terrified, I wipe my face only to find that no tears have been shed.

As soon as I close my eyes again, I return to the hospital. My feet pound the ground as I race through the labyrinthine corridors of my nightmare, desperate to catch up to my mom. Her figure wavers like a mirage in the distance, but each time I draw closer, she disappears into thin air.

The night turns into an endless stream of terror, each nightmare building on the last.

I wake up tired and agitated but also with the strange

comfort of knowing why my mother withheld her affection. I wasn't to blame for her difficulties. My heart feels as if it's about to burst out of my chest with a deluge of emotions: fury, despair, agony, hope, relief, and ease.

There's a knock on my door.

"I want to sleep, please," I groan.

"No, you ain't, sis. You're coming out of your girl cave because I prepared a delicious full English breakfast." Eli pauses. "Can I come in?"

"Okay," I mumble.

He pulls the chair up to my bed and tucks my hair behind my ear. "Dwelling on the past is only valuable if it helps propel you forward, sis."

One side of my mouth curves up a little. "You made breakfast?" I ask, intrigued. Eli isn't known for his cooking skills. The best he can do is make toast with peanut butter. But something does smell delightful.

"It's waiting for you." He winks.

"I'll get up in a few minutes."

"Okay, sis." He leaves.

I pull the duvet over my head for a few minutes. Then I hear him call my name. I forgot how relentless he can be.

"We're waiting!"

"Okaaay, I'm getting up."

I sit up, growl, and close my eyes when I see the letter on my table.

After plunging myself into the bathroom, I stare at my reflection in the mirror. Who is this swollen-faced, hollow-eyed woman?

After showering, I walk into the kitchen and immediately want to retreat like a little lamb. I see a wolf—a few wolves.

Jay is smiling at me.

My brother extends his hand. "Come sit. Let's have breakfast. I was only helping. Jay prepared it, so it's edible. Promise."

I clasp his arm, wondering if I'm hallucinating. Sarah and Luke are also in the kitchen. There are tiny daisies in the middle of the table and five empty plates.

I often fantasized about this sort of gathering, but it seemed too far-fetched to ever happen. Luke and Sarah would never choose to hang out together outside of work, my brother lives far away, and Jay doesn't associate with the other two. Plus, Sarah and Luke probably have a very low opinion of me. So I'm at a loss as to why we're all having breakfast together.

"Good to see you, sweetheart," Sarah says.

Oh dear. I need to stop staring and speak. Eventually, I muster a few words. "It's good to see you too."

Jay serves the food. He's parboiled sage sausages and seared them on high heat to get the crispy casing. He's also cooked beans, and it looks as if he's seasoned them with a spoonful of mustard.

"The sunny-side up, aka British fried egg for Dasia!" he says with a smile, placing an egg on my plate, along

285

with brown-butter-drenched mushrooms and warm, buttery, caramelized cherry tomatoes.

I watch everyone dive in then catch Sarah's eye. The power of her kind and soft gaze is so strong that I instantly feel as if she can see all the pain I hold deep inside. She smiles. I try to control it, but I suddenly start sobbing. I haven't cried since before reading the letter.

Sarah jumps up and puts her arms around me.

"I'm so sorry, Sarah." I look around the table. "So sorry, everyone."

"Shhhh, let's have a lovely breakfast together."

I nod, and she releases me from her arms.

I gobble the food and end up cleaning my plate before anyone else.

Jay smiles. "Someone was hungry."

"You make the best breakfast ever."

I blink when Luke speaks for the first time this morning. "You haven't tried my breakfast yet." He's looking at his plate, munching away as though he didn't just touch my heart.

With that three-letter word, I feel a sense of hope. *Yet.*

Then it hits me like a ton of bricks—he's not to be trusted.

I feel a surge of anger and disappointment, and for a moment, I want nothing more than to despise him. But I find myself unable to do so. Perhaps I'm just too drained to harbor hatred.

Sarah and I move into the living room after breakfast,

and I can hear the others in the kitchen. I sit back and listen to the banter among the three significant men in my life.

Two, not three, I remind myself. *Two!*

A few minutes later, Luke appears with a mug in each hand. "Finely brewed coffee for the lovely ladies." He hands me one with the words *A Hug in a Mug* on it.

I smile and look up to see him watching me. My walls want to recede, but I hold on to them.

"We got them, Dasia," he says. "Your trap helped, and no patient was harmed."

"I know," I mumble. "Sarah called and updated me."

"And these mugs are from Roy. He sends his love."

I look at the pretty mug. As thoughts of Roy flood my mind, a sense of lightness takes over. I can't help but smile, recalling how I used to be confused about my feelings toward him. That chapter of my life is now behind me. He's a wonderful friend, that's all.

A few fresh tears stream from my eyes.

Sarah places her hand on my arm. "What a way to catch them, Dasia. You're big news at work."

My eyes widen and my heart starts racing, but I quickly remind myself that this time round, the news is positive. It's about how I helped.

I look at Sarah. "I'm just so happy no patient was harmed."

Instead of writing to my brother, I sit across from him and talk to him.

"What was that about?" I ask. "How come Sarah and Luke joined us for breakfast on a Saturday morning?"

"Luke and Sarah were here, having breakfast with us, and you're curious about why they came on a Saturday? I thought you were a genius, but I may have given you too much credit."

I throw a cushion at him. "You know what I'm asking. What were they doing here?"

"They told Jay that they wanted to see you, so Jay invited them over for breakfast. He wanted it to be a surprise for you. He didn't tell me either, so when they turned up this morning, I was shocked too.

"I looked like a mess."

"That's all right. When you really care about someone, you love every part of what makes them who they are. That includes weepy eyes, a swollen nose, and puffy cheeks.

"Oh, no, Elias!" I cover my face with my hands in embarrassment.

He pulls my hands away. "Listen, you're gorgeous. I don't know how you did it, but everyone here seems to really care about you even though you only met them seven months ago."

Excitement flickers in his eyes. "That Luke guy is trouble," he says with a chuckle. "He contacted Jay to see how you were. Jay mentioned that I was coming, and he then got hold of my number. When we were exploring London with Jay, he bribed us with beer and held us hostage. He interrogated us about you."

"Did he? How did he even know how to reach Jay?" I ask, feeling my cheeks getting warmer.

"Social media. And that pub didn't even have a good IPA."

"What did he ask about?"

"I say he's a keeper."

"Very funny, but he's not mine to keep."

Suddenly, a wave of icy dread washes over me, and I can feel my face becoming cold. The emotional turmoil that Luke ignites within me is utterly exhausting. It's like being on a never-ending roller coaster of feelings. I must get off this ride.

"He's racing to become just that," Eli says.

"I don't think so. It was nice to see him here, but he has a girlfriend, remember? Emilia. And he's not who he appears to be." The sorrow I feel fills my entire being.

"That's very strange. I like him. He seems genuine." Then, looking at me with tender eyes, he asks, "Dasia, will you call or write to Mom?"

Now it feels as though the roller coaster I'm on has ascended to the very heights of the sky and is about to plummet down vertically.

"I'm not sure yet. It all feels too raw. I don't feel strong enough to process all her revelations."

"And that's fine. We can't be strong at all times. With

the ebbs and flows of life, experiencing the full range of emotions is just part of it."

I hold his gaze. "Will you share with me some of the ebbs and flows of your life?"

"Absolutely," he replies, grinning. "I was starting to think you'd never ask."

Chapter Thirty Seven

I love hearing Eli and Jay chatting in the kitchen, so I join them for a little while.

"You don't even fly, and you're here!" I can't help but squeal with delight.

"I think I'm now more frightened of not being able to fly as freely as I desire," he says. Having ventured beyond his comfort zone, he's already different.

With my coffee in hand, I retreat to my bedroom, where I find my eyes drawn to my mother's letter, still resting on the table. The raw, sore wound emerges as I grapple with everything she revealed. Nevertheless, I have the choice to embrace the future and forge ahead.

While I can acknowledge her pain, I still find it difficult to rationalize her behavior toward me. Maybe someday. But this won't have any bearing on my existence.

I reach for the journal my brother gifted me. There's a

beautiful daisy in pastel colors on the cover, and above it are the words *Write Your Own Story*.

My pen poised over the first page, I think for a moment then slowly write a sentence.

Happiness is a conscious choice!

After reading it aloud a few times, I ponder if life is something that happens to us.

Not at all! Do we have a part in forging our own path? In a word, yes!

Thoughts of the past few months flood my mind—the chances I took, the changes I embraced, the risks I faced. So many wonderful people showed up in my life.

A realization comes to me, and I write it down.

As you offer a humble dose of love, the universe responds by showering you with its own.

Giddy with joy, I gently cup my face in my hands. "Oh, my goodness!" I whisper. "I'm finally ready to live again."

I continue peeling back the layers of my existence with every stroke of my pen.

This is my life, and I own it. This life belongs to me, no matter which way it goes, whether upward, downward, or sideways. It's filled with choices that I alone make. No one other than me is responsible, or can be blamed, for the outcomes, since every path is full of decisions I make on my own.

I gently close my journal, allowing myself a moment of tranquility. A few minutes later, I hear a chime come from my cell phone. The tranquility prevails—until it doesn't. A message from Luke.

> Hi, it was good seeing you yesterday. We still need your help with the automation. This time as a computer-science engineer, though. Did you see the incident reports? Call me so we can coordinate our schedules for the week ahead.

Sarah brought me my work laptop yesterday, and I read all the incident reports about the hackers, as well as reports about the company's plans to improve cybersecurity. The hospital staff had been perplexed and outraged, but no patients were injured.

After numerous cycles of staring at my phone, placing it on the table, then picking it up again, I finally dial Luke's number. To my surprise, he picks up almost instantly, as if he were waiting for the call.

"Dasia, great that you called. We need your input to strengthen the system so it blocks malicious network traffic."

I'm silent, unsure of what to say.

"Dasia, Tanya tells me you're beyond skilled as a software engineer."

I keep my cool. "But I did lie on my CV."

"Yes, you did. But you also fixed a huge catastrophe. Our cybersecurity had ongoing issues before you arrived. And you took serious risks with the dark web."

A gripping stillness takes over me.

"Dasia." He pauses. "Roy told me you looked so broken when he found you by the river but that you had a raging fire in your eyes, that they were bright and alive."

"Why was he there?"

"I called him and asked him to find you."

"Ah, I see."

"But the issue persists. Can we focus on that now? Will you help so we can prevent another crisis?"

I close my eyes. They feel like two burning coals. "Of course. Tell me what you want me to do."

"We're taking a break from the automation project for a few weeks, and Tanya is insisting that you start working with them this week."

"Sure."

"She claims she's never before witnessed such remarkable ability and skill. Apparently, you're a true genius among mere mortals."

"I'm glad she thinks so," I say, with a sigh of relief.

I spend the week programming and maintaining software applications. I once worked with algorithms, equations, and numbers on a daily basis, and there's so much freedom in simply being myself again. No longer do I feel the need to act differently or hide anything from anyone.

I'm just being me.

Sarah suggested that I continue to work remotely until my ankle fully recovers, so I dial into meetings with the cybersecurity team. We work in collaboration; everything is a joint effort.

On Saturday, Sarah and I meet for lunch. We picked a family-run teahouse close to my place. I arrive first and am happy to see a table by the window. There are a few tables outside, but I love the vintage decor inside, and the sweet smell of the freshly made cakes. Jay introduced me to this teahouse, and I've become obsessed with their cream tea.

Sarah walks in, and I wave at her from my seat. She opens her arms a few steps before reaching me, and I lean into her arms. We hug for a moment and then settle into our chairs.

"What a charming little place, a great pick," says Sarah. "I need to talk with someone, and there's no better listener than you."

"Of course. I'm always interested in hearing what you have to say."

Our server arrives, and we order two cream teas.

"The crises are under control," says Sarah, when we're

alone again, "but oh my gosh, Dasia, we're all in awe of your wonderful insights and actions. Our incident has made national news, and we made sure to thank you by name in our press release."

Once again, I've made headlines. My pulse is pounding and my chest feels tight, but I remind myself it's for a good reason this time. This time, my passion for technology proved useful.

Sarah looks at me cautiously. "I have something I want to tell you."

"Sure, I'm all ears."

"My husband and I had envisioned retiring together, but to my pleasant surprise, I was given a promotion. However, I find myself no longer excited about it."

"Really?"

"This executive position, it seems to stray too far from the front line. That's where my true passion lies." She casts her eyes downward.

"In retrospect, my instincts were calling me, and I should have listened. The gratification of improving things and preserving jobs is undeniable, but . . ." She looks out of the window. "I think this is what 'aspirational regret' is."

"What's that?" I ask, genuinely curious.

"It's when you desire something intensely, or believe that you do, but as time passes, you realize that you're not the same person you were when you first desired it. I remember my first day at Thames City Healthcare Group. I dreamed of one day being a top executive. But that was almost forty years ago."

"And you aren't the same person you were forty years ago," I say, nodding.

"Just like you're not the same person you were a few months ago, sweetheart."

Our order arrives. I pour our tea into the delicate bone-china cups and declare, "You're right. I'm different. I now get pleasure from tea."

When I open my eyes the next morning, I don't feel weighed down. Instead, I feel rather buoyant. When I reflect on my week, I can't help but grin. I worked as a computer-science engineer again. And then there was that great lunch with Sarah yesterday. On the day Eli was scheduled to fly back to the States in the late evening, I made a reservation for an afternoon tea experience for both of us to enjoy. It will be a perfect way to use the Christmas present vouchers that had recently resurfaced in the back of my drawer.

The scent of coffee sneaks into my bedroom, and the sound of my brother and Jay chatting is so comforting. I get up to join them.

"Good morning, you two," I say, walking into the kitchen in my pajamas. "What do you have to talk about so early in the morning?"

"Our favorite subject is you, of course," Eli says.

"I'd better join the conversation to correct some facts, then," I say, as I sit in a chair next to them.

Jay gets up and makes me a coffee without asking if I want one or how I take it. It's lovely when another human being gets you, knows what you want at certain hours, and wants you to have an awesome start to the day. Jay is one of those rare friends, if you're fortunate enough to have one, who genuinely cares and understands the little things that bring you happiness.

I sip my coffee as my brother declares, "We're going for a canal walk. It's a beautiful Sunday."

"Have a lovely time," I say, hiding my disappointment. I don't want to stay home alone today.

"No, no, no!" Jay says. "You're also coming. Since you're already off work tomorrow. And who knows, we may bump into Luke." He grins. "I told you months ago he has the hots for you."

"No, he doesn't. He has a girlfriend! Could I enjoy my coffee without you putting strange thoughts in my head?"

Next thing I know I find myself in my walking shoes taking the train to King's Cross. Jay explains that the Regent's Canal Walk is a treasure of London, as the waterway winds through parks, bridges, the zoo, and vibrant neighborhoods.

"We have our own Little Venice in London," Jay coos. "Let's walk there."

When we reach Little Venice, I feel elated. Two canals converge into a picturesque basin. I look at the boats, the plants, the walls, and the green water reflecting the willow trees. I hear my brother and Jay chatting in the distance. Harmony is to know and appreciate everyone's singular contribution to the whole. Everything matters in this stunning picture.

I feel a deluge of emotions. Happiness is stronger when it's shared with others. The burden of sadness also lightens when we share it with other people. During the last few months, I discovered that we grow when we take risks to protect others. Our hearts expand when we bring joy to others.

Growing up, I learned to hide. I never felt part of a whole. Over the last few months, the people in my life, with their love and support, have helped me discover the woman I've kept hidden. I finally feel that I'm part of a whole, and that my contribution is as significant as any other person's. I matter.

Chapter Thirty-Eight

On Tuesday, I got up at my usual hour, as if I were going to the office. I even prepared my outfit the night before. My ankle feels much better, but Sarah insisted I keep taking it easy.

Eli left yesterday, and I'm already missing him. It feels as if he were around for twelve seconds, not twelve days.

The doorbell rings. I open the door and see a young man holding a vibrant bouquet featuring bursts of orange roses, pink snapdragons, and bright golden craspedia.

"Flowers for Dasia," he says with a smile.

I thank him, take the flowers, and rush to get some change for his tip before checking the small card.

Have a wonderful week.
  – Luke

I touch each flower with a heavy heart, wishing things

were different. I wish my heartbeats were lighter and happier.

I grab my phone.

> Thank you, they're colorful.

> You're welcome. Can you call when you have a minute?

I look at his message, and my thumb hovers over the call button.

> I'll call in a while.

After some time, I sit in front of my laptop trying to focus on my work, but all I can do is stare at the blank document on my screen. I need to call Luke and get it over with.

I become sad and nervous as soon as I pick up the phone. *Just say thank you for the flowers, no biggie.*

I raise my chin and press the call button.

He answers almost immediately. "Dasia."

"Luke."

"Do you have plans Sunday afternoon?"

Thunderstruck by his question, I'm silent for a moment, unable to find the words to express my despair. The world around me appears consumed with darkness. Then, with a voice as cold as winter frost, I whisper, "I have plans on Sunday."

That's it. All hope is now gone forever.

After a few seconds, he responds. "Uh . . . You do. Okay."

I change the subject, asking him a work-related question. We discuss it, and then he says, "We also need to update you on the vandalism issue, Dasia." He's gone back to his usual self.

"Sure," I say, feeling uneasy.

"Let me get Sarah, and we'll meet in thirty minutes."

"Okay, I'll call in."

I shake my head after hanging up, and with a stern face, I utter out loud, "Jackwagon schmuck, you don't get to ask a woman out when you hide a girlfriend who vandalizes that woman's belongings."

But my attempt to get angry doesn't work. My heart sinks deeper and deeper. I feel like a deflated balloon.

When I join the meeting, Sarah starts by saying, "Dasia, about the vandalism. Luke confronted the woman from the HR department, and she was suspended immediately."

"Yes, I know. It was Luke's girlfriend."

"What?" they both ask at the same time.

"Uh . . . Sarah, you mentioned that it was Luke's girlfriend."

"She was never my girlfriend," Luke says, his voice raised with irritation, his eyes wide. "We only had one date. It was one meal a few months ago."

Sarah chimes in. "I was in a hurry when I called you, Dasia, and quite upset about everything. On top of it all,

Luke had mentioned that they dated a few months ago, and I was furious about his judgment."

Huh. I feel the blood rush to my cheeks.

"Also," says Luke, "a few weeks ago, I received photos of you and one photo of both of us with a threatening note. I immediately reported it to the police and our HR department."

I gasp and then exhale. I didn't see the note, only the photos. How wrong I was to think he was a sneaky stalker.

"We know she left a threatening note on your desk too," says Luke, shaking his head and gazing down for a beat.

"Yeah. I suspected that it would be the same person who ruined my coffee station."

Luke's intense eyes fill my screen. "Out of the blue, she would suddenly appear, insisting on another date, whether it was in the office kitchen or other locations. Initially, I made an effort to explain that there wouldn't be any more dates. I tried to maintain a friendly distance, but I never would've guessed that she'd escalate things to this level. Her behavior grew increasingly obsessive."

I like this Luke, the troubled one who attempts to convince me.

"I'm sorry, Dasia," he adds.

"Okay." Though I appear calm and together, my heart is doing flips despite my best efforts to disregard its elation over what Luke is saying.

Sarah looks at Luke and then turns to the screen. She has a determined look in her eyes. "Now we need all our energy together to cross that ocean. We're in the last few stages of the automation project, and we're close to saving all the jobs with the efficiencies we've created. Complaints are down, and patients are happier. But we still need to get the final approval for the full implementation."

"I'm in," I say.

Luke smiles. "Excellent!"

"But what about my misleading CV and the fact that I didn't disclose the inquiry?" I ask. "What's the HR policy on that?"

"Leave that with me," Sarah says. "But I have a bone to pick with you for not disclosing your incredible skills and credentials. Although you did make my life a lot easier with your fast solutions."

Luke interjects. "If I'd known of your capabilities, Dasia, I would have included you in many of my earlier plans to make the automation project successful. You didn't have to travel alone on this journey."

I fix my gaze on him and then on Sarah. "You're right. I should have been honest, but I assumed you'd judge me and wouldn't want to work with me. I didn't think I'd have a chance if I told you. I didn't think I had another option."

"There's always another option," says Sarah. "It's rarely a case of either-or."

I smile then shift my attention to Luke. "I didn't believe you were fully invested in this." I pause. "I'm still unsure. I overheard you and Mr. Goodwin having hushed conversations and discussing confidential reports that Sarah was unaware of."

Enough is enough, I think, once again steaming with anger.

Sarah gives a little smile and raises her brows. "But I did know all about that, Dasia. Luke reported everything to me."

"What?" Confusion replaces my anger.

"We have some news on Mr. Goodwin too," she continues. "There was a vote of no confidence in him by the board last week. He doesn't care about a single soul here. In fact, he may even be charged. We found out he was working with an investor to take down the South London Outpatient Hospital so they could buy it cheaply. There's an investigation happening."

"Oh wow. I knew he didn't care, but wow."

Sarah goes on. "When we heard he was our new CEO, we wanted to gain his trust, and Luke working closely with him was part of this. Having heard about his vile personality and how manipulating he could be, Luke and I formulated our own little strategy. Mr. Goodwin has a reputation for not working well with female leaders, so we decided to push Luke into the firepit. Luke pretended to be his confidant, but he told me everything along the way."

"Like, everything?" I ask. "Even that Mr. Goodwin suggested that the automation project should be led by you, Sarah, so that if it failed, you'd be held accountable and lose your job?"

She grins. "That too. I know you tried to warn me about that right at the beginning."

I look at the screen in shock.

"We've made Dasia speechless, Sarah," Luke says, and they both chuckle.

"So I wasn't the only person keeping secrets and trying to present a certain image to others," I say, with relief.

They both nod with smiles on their faces.

Luke adds, "Seeing his disregard for female leaders and having to listen to his ageist remarks . . ." He shakes his head. "It was hard not to punch him."

"Especially when he called you *son*," Sarah says with a laugh.

"Ah yeah, that was killing me slowly."

I'm at a loss for words, feeling too stunned to process the revelation that Sarah was involved all along and Luke wasn't stabbing her in the back. Instead, they were playing their own game in a world of ruthless gamers.

"Okay," Luke continues. "Here's my last confession of the day. When you were contemplating whether to take the project-assistant job, I put the other applicants' files on your desk. Remember that day?"

I nod. I remember it vividly indeed.

"They were empty files. I didn't look for another applicant."

"I remember your smirk when I told you I'd stay. That's why!"

"I had no idea!" Sarah says.

I suddenly remember Luke's conversation with Sarah's husband and realize there must be an explanation for that too. I hope there is. But I'll have to set that aside for now —I've already had enough surprises for one hour. And I don't want to expose personal information that Sarah might not have shared with Luke.

Sarah's blue eyes are as bright as the sky after a storm. "Now, we still have jobs to save, patients to make happier, a project to complete. So here's the plan."

She outlines the tasks and activities of the next few weeks.

At the end of our conversation, I say, "Thank you for giving me another chance."

"You gave yourself that chance, love. You manifested it by starting to believe in yourself and taking action. I'm overjoyed that you did. Belief in oneself is the first step to success, happiness, a fresh start, or second chances in life. It begins there."

Just before we end the meeting, I decide to take another chance.

"Umm . . . Luke. I am free on Sunday afternoon."

His vast grin is comical, and Sarah's eyes crinkle with a warm and genuine smile.

After the virtual meeting, my mind repeats the same sentence over and over. *She was never his girlfriend!* I even add a little melody to it.

"Someone's flying high in the sky," Jay says, as he walks out of his bedroom. "What's happening?"

"Nothing." But I'm unable to stop my grin from spreading.

"Anything to do with one of the dashing brothers?"

"Might be."

"Which one?"

"C'mon Jay! You know which one." But I know he won't let me off the hook so easily.

"I want to hear it from you, Sparkles. No judgment. Open your heart to me. True friendship's key ingredient is no judgment. So tell me from your heart. I'm always happy to listen to you talk about the dashing brothers."

I look into his caring eyes. "Okay, I'll admit it. I liked —or thought I liked Roy because he's a friendly, sincere, and safe person in a harsh and complicated world with secrets and lies."

"I must say, he has a pretty charming and attractive face too." Jay grins. "Those dark chestnut eyes would melt anyone, and don't get me started on those masculine arms."

I laugh. "Yes, he's pretty awesome. You know he never goes to a gym? He's just built like that."

"Is that so, Sparkles?"

"Yes, that's so, and he's a very close friend now."

"And anything else you wish to reveal?"

I wave my hand in front of his face as if wiping off his smirk. "You don't need any other revelations. You figured it all out already."

"Yeah, I figured it out months and months before you realized what all your nerves meant when you were around Luke.

"I know you did," I say, "Cause you're an awesome friend."

Jay suddenly stands and begins pacing. "So, I've another matter now. Jarrett and I are to meet." He clears his throat. "This evening. But remember, we want you to be there too."

"Copy that, loud and clear, sir," I reply, with a comical bow.

"Okay, no joke, you need to keep the peace between us."

"You have my attention . . . sir!"

"I'm serious, Dasia."

"Same here," I whisper. "Your Highness."

I can see how anxious Jay is, likely because he's wounded and because he genuinely cares. It occurs to me that occasionally, our negative feelings arise because of our emotional connection to someone or something.

Maybe not all bad emotions are necessarily bad, I think. *Maybe they're just the heart's way of communicating with us.*

That evening, I find myself wedged between Jay and Jarrett at the bar of the local pub. They insisted on sitting side by side instead of at a table, so we're lined up beside each other. I can sense the tension between them; they wear sulky expressions. But I can't help but detect love for each other in their eyes, however much they try to hide it.

"So. Where are you from, Jarrett?"

"Birmingham."

Of course he is. I try again. "Do you visit London often?"

"I live here." He steals a glance at Jay.

"Oh, you do," I say.

Can love open even the most securely fastened doors? Is it powerful enough to mend even the most shattered friendships?

I excuse myself to go to the washroom. When I come out, I see them deep in conversation over the empty chair between them. I study them a beat. They're here not because they're upset with each other. They're here because of their love for each other. Nothing else matters.

A broad grin spreads across my face.

Not everything needs to be resolved immediately. One step at a time.

And they took that first step.

Chapter Thirty-Nine

I t's finally Sunday morning. Excitement surges through my veins with every passing minute as I get ready for my picnic date with Luke. He's picking me up at 1:00 p.m.

"I like this guy," I mutter, feeling a nervous flutter in my stomach when I hear the doorbell at 12:55 p.m. I take one last look at myself in the mirror. Then, at full speed, I head to the door and throw it open.

He's handsome in a pair of navy chinos and a matching knit shirt. His light-brown coat suggests that it's overcast outdoors. The forecast says showers, but it matters not, for I'm armed with my raincoat and will embrace whatever comes my way.

"You look radiant and picnic-sophisticated," he says, eyeing me.

"Let's have a picnic, then."

"Is Jay home?"

"He's not, but if you want him to join us, I can text him," I say mischievously.

He chuckles then leads me to his car. As he graciously opens the passenger door for me, I pause for a moment, meeting his gaze, and then step in.

When we approach Hampstead Heath, Luke circles a few times before finding a parking space. He gets out and opens the trunk, and my eyes widen in delight. "Oh, this is the cutest picnic basket I've ever seen."

"So cute picnic baskets ignite a spark in your eyes. Good to know." He then opens the double lid, and I hold my hand over my mouth.

"Look at these treats!"

Next, he opens his jacket to reveal tickets peeking out of the inner pocket. "Take them."

"Oh wow, we're here for a classical music concert! How wonderful." I hug him, too excited to stop myself.

We walk into the park and situate ourselves. The sky is growing darker, but we have an umbrella, too. No better place than London to have a romantic picnic in the rain.

"Do you bring women here often?" I ask.

"No, Dasia, this is the first time. And for your information, I didn't already own a double-lid willow picnic basket with a red-and-white-plaid lining, as well as the plates, wine glasses, and utensils that came with it. But I can show you the receipt that proves I purchased it a few hours ago."

"You certainly know how to sweep a girl off her feet."

"I may have had a little help from someone tall, dark,

and handsome." He peers at my shocked face. "And you look adorable when you're confused, with those big eyes." He gives a hearty chuckle. "I'm talking about Jay."

"What? Jay helped you with all of this?"

"Yeah, if not for him, we'd be sitting on the lawn with premade sandwiches."

"That would still be lovely, but show me the receipt," I say teasingly.

"Seriously?"

"Yes." I am curious.

He takes out his wallet and hands me the receipt.

I gasp. "Over four hundred pounds!"

"Yes, Jay said that under no circumstances could we have a picnic without one of *these* baskets."

I laugh. "He's the best."

Soon, the concert starts, but twenty minutes in, lightning and deafening thunder interrupt it.

"Nothing to worry about," Luke says, opening the large umbrella. "I'm well prepared."

"Was this also Jay's idea?"

"Nope, I've just lived in this beautiful city long enough."

We enjoy the closeness under the umbrella for only a few minutes. Then the wind picks up and the raindrops come at us from the side rather than the top.

In less than ten minutes, we're drenched and our picnic setting is thoroughly wet. We throw everything into the basket and run back to the car, every piece of clothing clinging to our skin. My foot lands in a puddle, and I start laughing uncontrollably. Luke joins me. How long has it been since I laughed so wholeheartedly?

When we reach the car, I don't get in. Instead, I stop and look up, opening my arms. The rain pours down, and the droplets cling to my face. Luke stands in the rain and watches me.

Finally, it feels as if spring has arrived in my life. It's been a long wait, and now, I can sense joy in almost every sphere of my life.

When we finally get in the car, we can barely see anything through the heavy rain. "Best to hold tight for five to ten minutes," Luke says. "Let the rain ease up. This was meant to be a summer drizzle, for cryin' out loud."

We watch the raindrops in silence for a while. Then Luke blurts, "I can't believe we only have a few more weeks to finalize the project." His words rush out like the torrential downpour.

"Yes," I say with a smirk. "Time to say adios."

He turns his body toward me. "No one is saying adios —I can tell you that." His eyes are fixed on me and his fingertips starts gliding through my hair.

"Is that an order, boss?"

This is the first time I've called him boss.

"It's me asking to be part of your life, hoping to be with you every day of your life."

Leaning toward him, I rest my head on the car seat and gently shut my eyes. I sense the gentle brush of his hand on my hair. "This feels good," I mumble.

"I'm aware," he responds softly. "I've watched your

hands caressing your hair countless times and I've dreamt of running my fingertips through, just like this," he whispers as if the intensifying rain itself echoes his words. Then there's a loud crack of thunder. A serene feeling washes over me. Keeping my eyes closed, I take a deep breath, savoring the moment of tranquility and warmth within the storm. It's a reminder that things aren't always what they appear to be.

When lightning flashes, I murmur, "Fall like a thunderbolt."

Luke's eyes light up. "You already did, Dasia. Right in the center of my life, and I'm never letting you go."

It feels as if a tidal wave of hope spills out of his heart and fills mine. A soft smile spreads across my face while my heart trips over its next beat, and then the next.

Chapter Forty

Today is the day. We've officially handed over the automation project to a full-implementation team. We received a glowing review from our finance and customer-experience teams. The project exceeded our expectations: the numbers look healthier than anticipated and job losses are no longer on the table. Sarah and I are in a celebratory mood.

"Let's go to Pages and Beans," Sarah says.

When we enter, I see Roy and Luke talking. They both beam when they notice us.

"I was just telling him not to mess this up," Roy says, winking at me.

Sarah and I nestle onto the bench at their table.

"Behave, little brother," says Luke.

"Dasia is very dear to me." Roy looks at me.

"Thank you," I mouth, with a grin.

"And wow. Waiting for you two to accept your feelings

for each other! Man, that was exhausting. I could use a vacation!"

Luke tries to shush Roy, but he continues. "The very first week you arrived, I knew my brother was head over heels for you. And when I saw how you looked at him a few weeks later, I realized no one else had a chance."

That explains why Roy pulled away at the cycling event.

Roy looks at me with intensity. "I was convinced my brother was married to his work until he met you, Dasia. Now I've got myself a great friend and a future sister-in-law."

"Stop it!" Luke and I both shriek, and then we look at each other, smiling.

Sarah chimes in. "All of us caught on long before you two finally confessed your feelings."

Luke says, "I never doubted my feelings, right from the beginning."

I'm at a loss for words but filled with warmth and comfort.

"What a journey this was," Sarah says. "So, I have news, well, an update to share with you all. My husband, after he retired, lost his sense of identity, and it was hard to be around him. So I worked even longer hours. Our distance from each other grew. But he's my husband of 38 years."

She pauses, and Luke and I look at each other. We've already discussed that we need to tell Sarah what her husband asked Luke. Unfortunately, there's no easy way.

Luke makes an attempt. "Umm, Sarah . . . On that note, I have something to tell you."

A small smile plays at the corner of her mouth. "I know, Luke. He told me."

We stare at Sarah with wide eyes. She continues. "Yes, he told me. He told me he'd done a terrible thing, trying to stop me from working. But he also told me, Luke, that you advised him to stop interfering and be proud of me. You told him he has a wonderful wife and he'd lose me if he continued acting this way."

Luke looks relieved.

I place my hand on Sarah's shoulder. "So how are you now?"

"I don't know yet. He made a big mistake. He's certainly in the doghouse. But he's still the man I fell in love with—he's not a bad person. We share a life, in good times, bad times, and retirement times." Her eyes glisten.

"He said he felt like he lost his sense of purpose after retiring. He's getting professional help, and I'm pleased about it."

Sarah looks at the table for a moment. "Life is full of ups and downs. But sometimes we skydive to the bottom. My husband didn't manage his downward fall well. But he knows this, now. He could have asked for my help before his crash landing, but I love him enough to help him find his way back because he accepts his mistake. The way people come out of a crisis shows who they are. And he's coming out of it humbly and with grace. So who knows, we might return to Hawaii, like we've always dreamed about."

Tears of relief and happiness fall from my eyes, and I don't brush them away.

"Second chances," I say.

"And then some." Sarah laughs. "Sometimes, you must take many chances to get what you want. We make mistakes, and we learn how to do things differently through these slipups."

"What about work, Sarah?" I ask.

"For now, I've proposed to the board that I reduce my working days. They've agreed to create a shared job role. We'll recruit another executive who wants to work part-time. And my office will be at the hospital site, not the head quarter. My husband will stay with me in London and cook our dinners on workdays. He's been attending cooking classes and seems to be developing a talent for it."

Luke leans in and touches my hand lightly and smiles at Sarah. "Hawaii sounds just wonderful." Then he looks at me. "Right, Dasia?"

He continues. "By the way, I have news too."

Roy interjects. "Me too, me too."

"You first!"

"No, I insist—you go!"

"I resigned," Luke blurts. "I've officially started my three months' notice period."

Sarah stands and hugs Luke with a proud smile. I admire how serene they look.

"You'll do wonderful things with your life, son," Sarah says, and steals a glance at me.

Roy hugs him, too. "Finally, man. It's time for you to do what you want in life." He looks at me. "You know this brother of mine started working so he could support our mum and me. He set his dreams aside almost twenty years ago."

I nod. He focused on his work and success because he had the responsibility of caring for his family. I'm so proud of him.

"You're leaving your job," I say, also rising to hug him. "That's a big step."

"My destination in life changed—finally." He winks at me.

"You can finally write that book now!" Roy exclaims.

My heart roars with joy, and then I blink. "Did he just say 'write that book'? "Are you planning to write a book?"

"Let's hear Roy's announcement first," Luke says.

Roy looks at Luke with admiration before speaking. "Okay, here it is. I finally made travel plans, for six months, and Mum agreed to join me. 'Cause I'm her favorite son," he says with a smirk.

We all stand again, lining up to hug and congratulate Roy.

"But who will run the café?" I ask.

"This gentleman here," he says, pointing to Luke. "He's taking over in three months. He'll run the café and start writing that book he always dreamed about."

"I'll run it until you return in six months, mate."

"You own half of it anyway. It's time for you to take some responsibility." Roy laughs.

I sit again and study Luke and Roy, the last two people on Earth that I would have expected to own a café together. Life is full of surprises.

I feel strong hands on my shoulders and look up to see Jay standing behind my chair. "You can't have a celebratory afternoon without me," Jay says cheerfully.

I hug him, and we all squeeze together to make space for him at the table.

"Luke is going to write a book, Jay," I chirp. I can't contain my excitement.

"I knew he was a creative type!" Jay looks just as thrilled as I am.

Luke takes a journal out of his bag. It's the one I saw in his drawer. "I began writing in this journal a few years ago, and things were going well for a while, but then I hit writer's block—until a few months ago, when I had a breakthrough."

"Oh, the things that love can do to you," says Roy.

Luke shoots his brother an evil but funny look. He then flips the pages of the journal, and we all reach for it, but he puts it back in his bag. "You'll have to wait to read it when it's published. But you won't have to wait long—I've already worked with editors and have a release date."

We all talk over each other.

"Love betters humans and boosts creativity," Jay says.

"I'm so proud of you, son," Sarah says.

"This is awesome, Luke." I squeeze his hand.

"Congratulations, pal!" Jay says with a wink.

I suddenly recall his password: Chapt3rone. Chapter One!

"I'm sure it's a real page-turner," says Roy. "I can't wait to read the first and last pages." He laughs, and it's infectious.

Joy spreads throughout the café.

Life is full of beautiful twists, curves, and turns. There's rarely a straight path.

I think of my family back home and my brother's unconditional love. My mother is trying her best to build a bridge between us. She called a few days ago, and we had a long conversation. Nothing earth-shattering, but it was good to hear her voice. I've stopped trying to figure out who's right and who's wrong and what happened in the past. I'm now more interested in how we can heal each other. But one step at a time.

The more my heart is filled with love and joy, the less it hurts. I look at my family in London, sitting around this table—the family I built. I thank life for the many second chances and then some.

Chapter Forty One

I step out of the office building overwhelmed with all the hugs I received. We had a small after-party; it's almost 9:00 p.m., and the sky maintains a soft glow. It's a beautiful July evening. Luke is outside the entrance waiting for me.

A breeze blows my hair across my face and mouth. He leans in and pushes the hair away. "Let's make this face visible." His eyes are luminous.

As we walk toward the Millennium Bridge, he takes my hand and laces his fingers with mine. I think of the bridges I've had to repair and the new ones I've constructed from scratch.

Beside this pretty stretch of the river, I've strolled at leisure, run in distress, and cried without hope. Now I walk beside it next to Luke as my heart beats like a hummingbird hopped up on caffeine. This river. It winds its way around several bends and curves, flows with beauty.

The bridge is bustling with people. The sky holds late sunset colors and a silver moon. We pause in the middle of the bridge and look out. "It's so beautiful," I say. "Look how the moon is situated."

I glance up at Luke, and my breath catches. His eyes twinkle. My smile widens as I take in the intensity of his gaze. Luke holds both my hands in his, never breaking his eye contact. He moves closer.

Before our lips connect, he whispers, "You are so beautiful. I'm already a moon in your orbit."

It's a kiss full of possibilities. My knees feel weak, and London starts to spin around me . . . *Swoon.*

Epilogue

Three months later

Luke sprints toward the park bench I'm sitting on. I set down my book. Earlier, I left him at home to finish editing his manuscript. He's waving something.

He runs up and immediately lifts me. We start spinning fast. I close my eyes, and the wind softly touches my skin. My hair floats.

When he puts me down, we're both a little unsteady on our feet.

"I missed you," he says, handing me an envelope. "This is for you."

I take out an official-looking letter. "What is it?"

"Don't know."

I read it with a bit of hesitation.

～

Dear Dasia,

   It is my great pleasure to invite you to attend our annual
Recognition Award Ceremony. Your contribution . . .

It's from the local member of parliament. As it happened, there were other hackers targeting numerous hospitals, and for the past few months, I've been assisting the healthcare department of the government to stop them.

"Wow, I'm invited to an award ceremony!"

A few weeks after the automation project was completed, I started working as an independent cybersecurity consultant. I've just signed a contract to work on sensitive and highly confidential government cases. I'm unable to say more on those. What I can say is that I'm seen. I'm also trusted, valued, and acknowledged.

Luke looks at me affectionately. "Yes, darling, and you absolutely deserve the recognition. And before the ceremony, we have a weekend plan."

As he unzips his lightweight jacket, I catch a glimpse of tickets tucked in his inner pocket.

"Take them."

My hands fly to my face. "Eurostar tickets to Paris!"

"We'll have a drink at the champagne bar to celebrate before we board," he says with a grin.

"And to celebrate your book, too," I say.

His book is about to be published! Just a few weeks ago, he gave me his manuscript to read. I delved into it, and it felt as if I could peer directly into the depths of the storyteller's soul. Truly a captivating tale that kept me turning the pages.

Luke cups my face and gazes into my soul. "Thanks for reminding me that we have more than one chance in all aspects of life."

I smile. "I've also learned that sometimes we need to give ourselves as many chances as possible to reach our dreams."

"You are my dream. This life is."

"Paris, here we come!" I shout, as he spins me around again.

I'm flying in his arms.

Shortly after I finished my contract at Thames City Healthcare Group, I moved in with Luke—we didn't want to spend another second apart. Not long after that, he got down on one knee on the Millennium Bridge and asked me to marry him.

"Yes! With all my heart and soul" was my immediate response. It felt as if everyone in London heard my loud YES and turned their heads in our direction.

My brother and mother were thrilled with our news, and we plan to visit them at Thanksgiving next month. Eli wants to discuss selling the family business when I visit. Our mother says she'll support us, whatever we decide. I know Dad would be proud of me.

I no longer need to yearn for a happy home. Luke and I have built one filled with the warmth of our love.

Our wedding will take place on a boat—our own Love

Boat. Roy will put a hold on his travels for a while, so he can be the best man.

Jay is on his own journey of self-discovery. The calligraphy app I created for him changed his life as an artist. He's become a social media phenomenon.

Sarah and her husband plan to spend more time in Hawaii; they were there for a few weeks last month. Since her relocation from the headquarters, she enjoys her role more, and she loves being right at the center of the hospital.

In less than a year, so much happened. I'm not the same person I was. I'm surrounded by people I love, I'm in love, and I know that I deserve this life.

Although my worth existed all along, I finally discovered it.

More from G.T. London

Check Out Book Two!

YES, I'm thrilled to announce that a beloved character from this story takes center stage as the hero of their own adventure in my next novel!

It will soon be available for pre-order.

G. T. London

Let's stay connected: Here are some great ways to stay connected and be the first to know about all things related to my writing journey.

Official Newsletter: Join my newsletter for updates on upcoming books, special deals, and events.
GTLondonauthor.com

Email:

gtlondon.author@gmail.com

Events: I'd love to meet readers in person. Please let me know of any literary events near you. I might be able to turn up—in person or virtually.

A Note From the Author

You, the lovely reader, I'm thankful that you gave a chance to a debut author.

I love reading and have always admired authors who craft beautiful, powerful stories and remarkable characters that can take readers into another world. I've often wondered what it must be like to have such a gift for writing a novel.

On October 17th, 2022, I gifted myself that opportunity and began writing my first novel. This was after attending a four-day writing seminar with my author husband. During this seminar, I learned that the first draft must be exclusively for the eyes of the writer and no one else.

I also realized that crafting a novel is an ongoing refinement and improvement process, and creativity flourishes with persistent practice. With final motivation by my husband's words, "Why don't you just write your first draft?" I completed my first draft in a mere four weeks.

Little did I know that the narrative of the first draft would change so drastically. I'd lose track of the countless edits, and the final version of the novel would be significantly different than the first draft.

Why am I sharing this? For the simple reason that I believe everyone has that gift to tell a story.

This has been a journey of tenacity filled with learning, plotting, brainstorming, reading, rewriting, editing, revising, refining, improving, and more editing.

Fast forward eight months, and I find myself overwhelmed with emotion as I pen this thank-you note to each and every one of you. Seriously, thank you, and thank you again!

Since then, numerous individuals have told me they have longed to write a book, written numerous chapters kept in a drawer somewhere, or even completed a full book that they've never published.

Let me tell you, it's within reach to to become a published author regardless of your background, age, education, or experience. And there's no better time than now to get started. *Why don't you just write your first draft?*

So here I stand, a leadership and business development coach, a guest lecturer, and now the proud author of a contemporary romance novel. The writing process is like a spool of ribbon: it rolls and grows, and the more you learn and practice, the better it gets. Then there is the journey of becoming an independent author and the exciting business of self-publishing.

Within a year, I am so close to achieving my dream of sitting at a table, surrounded by impressive piles of my own books, with fans lining up for their autographed copies. I'm ever so grateful.

But, above all, thank you for making my dream come true by reading this book. My most significant metric in writing? YOU! The reader. Your support means the world to me.

I would greatly appreciate it if you could leave a review on Amazon or Goodreads—it would mean a lot!

G.T. London

The Authorpreneur

Special Thanks

I'm an author!

This has been quite a journey filled with encouragement, support, and cheering from an army of friends, family, and the writing community each step along the way.

I've been fortunate enough to work with two exceptional editors.

Jodi Warshaw, with your help and direction, Dasia's story soared higher than I ever thought possible. Your initial edit letter — particularly the words of praise, "You've written a true page-turner" — will always stay with me. I learned so much from your direction, remarks, and suggestions; thanks to you, I am already a better writer.

Rachel Small, thank you for your support above and beyond and the several "haha" moments sprinkled throughout the manuscript; it added an extra layer of joy to my work. Your excellent input and keen eye for detail have truly improved the flow of the story.

A special mention to Cherie Chapman, the brilliant cover designer who patiently addressed all my queries despite being on the other side of the world, literally.

To my friends and family across the globe—the United States, the United Kingdom, Germany, Switzerland, Turkiye, and beyond—I cannot express how much your support has meant to me or how thrilled I am to see the pride that radiates from your eyes. Every one of you played a big part in my writing journey, and I will always be thankful. With you, I receive around-the-clock excitement and support, knowing that there is always someone by my side, no matter the time zone. How fortunate I am.

To my small but mighty ARC team, Jason and Lale, your support, and dedication are truly appreciated – thank you!

And, none of this would have been possible without the intense encouragement and help from my loving husband. Jason, I wouldn't have dared to dream so big if you weren't standing beside me. Having an author partner who also doubles as my writing friend, business collaborator, publisher, marketing strategist, videographer, web designer, learning companion, tech lead, proofreader, and so much more— I'm in awe of how you do it all, thank you very much! I am simply grateful to the universe that our paths crossed in London. I love you . . .

Are cities thanked in this case? Actually, I do. I thank London, where I've lived most of my adult life. This city holds a special place in my heart. It's where I found lifelong friends, took daring leaps, fell many times, got back up, ran toward my dreams, and grew into the person I am today.

The events of this novel and Dasia's tale take place in London, and I'm an author who will forever be a Londoner at heart.

And my eternal appreciation goes to **YOU**, the beautiful reader. Thank you

About Me

I believe that we should take as many chances as necessary to turn our dreams into realities.

For most of my adult life, I embraced the vibrant energy of the bustling city of London. I dedicated myself to making a difference as a healthcare improvement executive, trainer, and coach in both the UK and Canada.

I hold an MBA from Warwick Business School in the UK and have had the privilege of being a guest lecturer for MBA students.

Now a full-time writer, I have published articles for Entrepreneur and Training magazines.

As a mentor at business schools in the UK and Hawai'i, I find fulfillment in guiding and supporting the next generation of business minds and entrepreneurs.

Coming from a diverse background as a Turkish-British author, my journey took me through Germany, Turkey, the UK, and briefly living in Canada. Now, I call the tropical paradise of Maui, Hawaii, my home, with my husband and fellow author, Jason.

I love crafting life-affirming stories that sweep readers away to far-off lands, where dramas, twists, and unexpected turns unfold, just like life itself.

I'm currently writing my next book while also outlining the one that follows and plotting the one after that.

facebook.com/gtlondon.author

instagram.com/gt.london.author

amazon.com/author/gt.london

goodreads.com/gtlondon

bookbub.com/authors/g-t-london

linkedin.com/in/gulcantelci

tiktok.com/@gt.london.author

Made in the USA
Las Vegas, NV
21 September 2023

77879579R00190